THEN HANG
ALL THE LIARS

Books by Alice Storey

First Kill All the Lawyers
Then Hang All the Liars

THEN HANG ALL THE LIARS

ALICE STOREY

POCKET BOOKS

New York London Toronto Sydney Tokyo

An *Original* Publication of POCKET BOOKS

POCKET BOOKS, a division of Simon & Schuster Inc.
1230 Avenue of the Americas, New York, NY 10020

To the Janes

Chelius
Danna
and Rottenbach

with love and gratitude

Special thanks to Dr. Kenneth Alonso, Chief Medical Examiner, State of Georgia, Carmen Alonso, Gary Bradley, and Dana Isaacson. Also to the Virginia Center for the Creative Arts, its director, William Smart, and staff. And once again, to Harvey, who always takes my calls.

Macbeth, Act IV, Scene ii:

Son: Was my father a traitor, mother?

Lady Macduff: Ay, that he was.

Son: What is a traitor?

Lady Macduff: Why, one that swears and lies.

Son: And be all traitors that do so?

Lady Macduff: Every one that does so is a traitor and must be hanged.

Son: And must they all be hanged that swear and lie?

Lady Macduff: Every one.

One

"May I pour you some tea?" Felicity Edwards Morris laid her still-beautiful hand upon the swan-neck handle of a silver teapot.

"Why, yes, please." Randolph Percy smiled.

God, he loved pretty women, and Felicity certainly did qualify as one. Never topped a hundred pounds in her whole life. She was like a white-haired, seventy-two-year-old, pansy-eyed doll who didn't look a day older than he, who was very well preserved if he did say so himself, at sixty-five.

"I never saw a bit of sense in lying about one's age," she'd offered the night Margaret Landry had introduced them at a dinner party. "Do you?"

Well, of course, she wouldn't—not a woman who'd kept her looks as well as Felicity, growing a patina like fine old silver as the years passed.

Which reminded him. He took a harder look at the teapot in her hand. Now that was worth a pretty penny. And there was plenty more of the good stuff on a breakfront in her parlor, and in the dining room he had made note of a dinner service for twenty-four, not to mention a huge beveled-glass cabinet filled with porringers, candle snuffers, salvers, chafing dishes, trays from toast to turkey, a sea of miniature salt and pepper shakers, and gravy boats.

"What *lovely* things you have." His porcelain caps were as white as Felicity's Haviland teacup.

"They say that my great-grandmother's having buried the silver in the back yard, so the Yankees wouldn't get it, gives it that special glow."

Felicity tilted her head as she delivered the line. Scarlett couldn't have done it better if she'd been here on this Sunday afternoon. And then she laughed her magical laugh that sounded like someone running a finger first up and then down a piano. Felicity's voice was only part of her very attractive package, the kind of package to which Randolph was always drawn: age, beauty, and, as he liked to say, the good things of life in plenitude. Or, in short, cash.

"Now look what Louise has put together for us." Felicity leaned forward from the green settee and lifted an embroidered cloth to reveal a feast that made Randolph sit up straight.

Lord knows, if there was one thing he liked as well as gambling and pretty ladies, it was good food. He rubbed his hands down his gray flannel pants while looking at two kinds of cheese, paper-thin Smithfield ham, bread-and-butter pickles, Louise's egg bread, to which he was most partial, marinated mushrooms, Vidalia onion relish which Felicity had canned, and homemade cookies—both chocolate lace and sand tarts.

"Felicity, I swear I've died and gone to heaven."

She smiled up at him from beneath her eyelashes, a trick practiced before her mirror and perfected sixty-five years ago. Then a glissando of her delighted laughter floated up as Randolph had pulled from behind his ear a silk orchid that he kissed and presented to her.

"You are so full of tricks! I don't know what I'm going to do with you."

He trained his lapis blue eyes on her soft violet ones.

"Marry me."

"Oh, Randolph! You are preposterous!"

"Now why do you say that every time I ask you? You know, Felicity, if I didn't think you were fond of me," he said and stuck out his bottom lip in what he'd always thought was an adorable pout, "I'd have my feelings hurt."

But he wasn't so upset that it put him off his feed. He piled a plate with ham and cheese and mushrooms while Felicity watched. Randolph had lovely table manners, but, my Lord, the quantity of food she'd seen pass through his lips, which he licked with the little eraserlike tip of his tongue and then wiped with his napkin. His fastidious gluttony made her tremble. What might that indicate about his other appetites?

"Well, my dear?" he asked between bites.

"Randolph, we've only just met."

"That is not true. It's been," he said and rolled mischievous baby blues as he calculated, "two months, four days, and sixteen hours. And in that time, I've come to love you as if I'd known you forever. My sweet, at our age," he said and leaned over, took her hand, and kissed it softly, "I'm afraid we don't have forever. *Carpe diem.* We must gather our rosebuds while we may."

Oh, it was tempting. He was such a clever man and so amusing. Why, she couldn't remember anyone who had made her laugh like Randolph—not since dear Joseph.

Pish! What was she thinking about? Joseph, who'd widowed her seven years ago, had never made her laugh. Why on earth was she so polite about him—even in memory—just as she'd always been the ever-so-proper banker's wife for, Lord have mercy, could it really have been forty-one years?

Why, that was silly. She wasn't even that old. She smiled and tossed her head. Felicity Edwards was still a young thing. With young passions.

Oh, Johnny. Her breath came faster. She crossed her bediamonded wrists across her breast so that her fingertips touched both sides of her throat. She felt her pulse there—quickening when Johnny entered the room. Johnny pushed her back on a pile of fur coats in the cloakroom of a Fifty-second Street speakeasy and ran his long, clever fingers along the scalloped edge of her rose silk teddy. Johnny sang into her ear the same tune she'd heard him play earlier that evening on his saxophone. Johnny thought she was the most talented ingénue on Broadway.

"You're not acting with me, are you, baby?" he teased as he tickled her ear with his pink tongue. She laughed. Lordy, how she laughed.

Look at him now, wiggling his ears. Her daddy used to do that when she and Emily were girls—gave them the silly giggles.

"Felicity?"

Her big soft eyes swam as she pulled herself back into the room and the present—wherever and whenever that was.

"I asked if you wanted to play cards."

"Oh, my dear!" She loved the past. It was so cozy. But the present was where she lived. Well, most of the time. "I must owe you five hundred dollars at gin. You are such a clever player. I don't know how I'm ever going to repay you." She dimpled then, for, of course, Randolph wouldn't take her money. It was all a game.

"I'm sure you'll find a way." Then Randolph lightly goosed her in the middle, just high enough to let her know that he was aware of her breast but low enough to call himself a gentleman.

For just a moment, his touch felt like Johnny's, and she began to drift again, but then she jerked herself back. *Pay attention.* "Why don't you do some card tricks for me? That's so amusing."

From Randolph's navy blazer sleeve, a deck materialized. He fanned the pasteboard royalty before her.

"Pick a card, any card."

Felicity's finger tapped. Her old rose-cut diamonds sparkled with blue fire. Tiffany & Co. He didn't have to guess their pedigree; he knew it.

If only it were so easy for him to pick winners at the track. He'd lost a bundle in Birmingham the previous week. Sea Breeze looked right, he smelled right, his jockey even wore the right colors. And what did the nag do? He stumbled and came in last.

Randolph cut and recut the cards, fanned and refanned, and out popped Felicity's choice. Queen of hearts.

She crowed with delight. They always did.

"I can't believe they taught you tricks like that at Harvard Law."

"How else do you think I worked my way through?" Randolph smiled. "As I've told you before, dear heart, my beloved father took a long walk off a short Savannah pier when he lost everything, leaving my poor mother without a dime, my sister without a dowry, and me in very embarrassing straits. Difficult to be genteel when you're all a-tatter. Of course, I'm grateful, dear sweet thing, that *you* never had to know about that sort of thing."

"Why, Randolph." It always embarrassed her when people

talked about money. She felt she ought to have Louise pack them a lunch. Or she should write them a check. Something.

"Now, Felicity. Remember I already know that except for the short time you were acting—up in New York—you've spent your whole life right here in Inman Park. Furthermore, this gorgeous piece of Victoriana," he said and waved a hand at the parlor in which they were seated, "is equally as elegant as the house on Elizabeth, in which you were born, surrounded with neighbors like the Candlers. Is it true that old Asa Candler kept the secret recipe for Coca-Cola in a vault in the basement of Callan Castle?"

"Gracious, I don't know. That's what everyone said, but I don't care about things like that."

"I know." She didn't have to. He put away the cards. "Enough tricks for now. Let's get out the Ouija and see what's in store for us on our trip." He pulled the Ouija board from beneath a table with long, slender legs carved like lilies. "I think we ought to take our time getting to Louisville, don't you? Take a couple of days to drive it. Spend the night in, say, Gatlinburg. The leaves should be beautiful by then. Let's see what the Ouija says. Put your fingers on the marker, dear."

Felicity did his bidding, and soon the electricity between them grew, and the plastic marker began to circle. She watched it slide around and around on the slick board. Was she really making it move, or was Randolph? Who knew? Who cared? It was a metaphor, she thought, for the dance that took place between a man and a woman when they stripped off their clothes, the dance that, when it was good, assumed a life of its own.

"Oh, Johnny," she began to sing. "Johnny be good to me."

"Hush now. You're interfering with the Ouija. You can't make it speak. You have to trust it."

"Oh, I don't have to make Johnny come to me." Felicity's voice grew huskier. It was a very sexy sound.

No wonder she was still in demand as a voice coach. She might be a little dotty, though that came and went, but to Randolph, her voice was a rush as thrilling as a bugle, as mournful as a dove. It was bright lights and promises and magic. It was rumpled sheets and fog horns and shiny golden rings.

"I just snap my fingers and Johnny's right there. There." She pointed.

Then Felicity stood—scattering the Ouija—and began to sway around the room, dancing to music that Randolph couldn't hear. But he could tell that in her mind someone was holding her, someone whom she loved.

"Yes, darling, anything you say," she trilled. "I'd go anywhere, do anything, if you play it for me. Pretty please. Play *Embraceable You.*"

Randolph could almost hear the horns in the background, that brassy sass of a big band.

He was tempted to get up and join Felicity—wherever she was. For a moment, he wondered if he really could.

He tucked the last piece of ham around the remaining bite of mushroom and washed it down with sherry, from a crystal decanter on the sideboard, which he helped himself to.

Could he whistle Felicity's tune? Wouldn't it be something if he could come in on the same note she was hearing out there in the ozone?

"Oh, Johnny," she cried in a long, slow moan, and the sound was royal blue flashed with fire-alarm red. Then it darkened through midnight blue, faded to purple. She flung her arms around her body as if she were holding together two halves that had been sliced apart.

"Johnny, Johnny, Johnny," she moaned. As the tears began to fall, her face crumpled. Fifty years twisted across her skin like a shroud.

"No!" Now her voice shrilled. It was an ugly sound. "No, no, you can't. I won't let you!"

Then the back door slammed, and the no-nonsense tones of Emily Edwards boomed through the house.

"What in the hell is going on?"

"Out." Emily pointed with one arm as she threw the other around Felicity's shoulders.

"I don't think it was anything I—"

"Mr. Percy, I'm sure that you're a perfect gentleman at all

times. But my sister is ill. She's not herself these days and I must ask you to leave." She pointed again with a finger that would brook no objection. "Now!"

Randolph Percy had little choice but to grab his hat.

Felicity pulled away from her sister and resumed her dance. It was a tearful fluttering now like a butterfly trying to get back outside a pane of glass.

"Embrace me," she whispered, a husky-voiced little girl. Then she hummed the song's old familiar tune.

"Felicity. Come sit down, darling." Emily patted the settee beside her. She reached out to her sister, but Felicity pulled away, needing both hands for her finale. She stood on an invisible stage, her arms raised beneath an imaginary spotlight that played across her lovely, ruined features.

"Don't be naughty. Baby, baby. Momma. Come to Momma." She faltered over the song's words, mixing them up, missing her cue.

"Oh, Felicity," Emily cried as the last note faded. "Poor Felicity." She enveloped her sister who relaxed—like a child who needed nothing more than a comforting hug. But only for a minute.

Then Felicity pulled back and spat, "You had to come in and ruin it, didn't you? You *always* do that. You *want* Randolph."

"Easy now. Easy. *Shhhhhh.*" Emily hadn't worked nearly fifty years as a nurse not to know how to deal with hysteria, though she knew this was only a symptom; Felicity's real problems were much more complex.

"No! There's nothing to talk about. You always send my boyfriends away. You're just jealous. You *hate* it that I'm the pretty one."

"I'm glad that you have admirers. I just wish you didn't get so upset."

"I'm *not* upset." Felicity flung out a hand, and a teacup crashed. "Look what you made me do!" Fresh tears flooded. "I don't know why you want all my boyfriends. You have plenty of your own. Too many." Then she lowered her volume to a whisper, a seething damp of menace. "Be careful, Emily. People are going to find out you're a slut."

Emily stood and smoothed her skirt. "I think, my dear, I'm going to get something to calm you."

"No!"

Felicity screamed and flailed with both fists now. The tea tray smashed onto the pink and green Chinese carpet.

"No! No! No! No! No!"

Emily made her way back to the little refrigerator in the pantry where she kept an assortment of medications for her spaniels, her own insulin, and, recently, Felicity's tranquilizers. Kneeling before it, she let her eyes unfocus, and there was Randolph Percy's face—the profile as handsome as a Roman coin, the still-full head of white hair. He was a handsome man with charm to burn. She could see why Felicity was so attracted to him, why she'd chosen to ignore the fact that he was about as trustworthy as a snake.

She unlocked the little refrigerator and reached inside.

What in heaven's name was she going to do about Felicity?

And what the hell was she going to do about Randolph?

She stared at the giant economy-size pharmacy bottle of Valium, which didn't need to be refrigerated but which she'd placed there for safekeeping. Then another handsome silver head swam into focus. George Adams. He was the man to call in a tough spot. She'd talk to her friend George. His niece Sam, too. Now she was thinking. Since Samantha Adams's series on the *Constitution*'s front page about that north Georgia sheriff, she'd been the talk of the town. Yes, Sam was what in her day had been called one smart, not to mention tough, cookie.

Tomorrow, Emily promised herself, she'd give the Adamses a jingle. Or maybe, with luck, she'd run into George tonight at Margaret Landry's party.

Two

In the middle of an opening-night party at the Players, a theater in Sweet Auburn just across the street from the Ebenezer Baptist Church and down the block from the first home of Martin Luther King, Jr., Sam Adams hid behind a potted palm. She was pretending to be a wallflower—actually more like a wall poppy in a bright red silk dress that did nothing to hide any of her considerable charms. She was sucking on a Perrier while she eavesdropped on two young girls.

"So when's Chill coming back from New York?"

The blonde who was asking had a lot of vinegar in her voice.

"Friday, Saturday—I suppose."

The *I suppose* was to let the blonde know she didn't really care, didn't give a hoot if Chill, whoever he was, was here or gone, and especially didn't care that this little bitch with the twenty-four-karat hair was getting to her. But she cared all right. This long, tall drink of iced café au lait cared a lot. She tossed her head, and her wavy mane of brindled brown and russet did a flip over a golden shoulder.

"So, what's the story? I thought you two were something, an item, you know, and here he's gone off to New York for three weeks."

"I told you already he's up there getting a gig together."

"A *what?*"

"A gig. A date at a rap club."

"Well, I guess I don't know about all that kind of thing, Laura."

Sam shot a quick look back to Laura, the one she was rooting for. The girl was some black, some white, maybe a tad of something else exotic, the kind of mix that comes out gorgeous, which is what she was. Green-eyed, golden-skinned gorgeous, and so slender in a chartreuse silk slip of a dress that Sam dropped the last bite of a cheese hors d'oeuvre she'd been holding into the potted palm.

"I know you don't know, *sugar,*" Laura said, getting into it now. The blonde was about to get burned. "They don't teach you Scotties nothing about *show* business, do they?"

The girl's range was something—from miming this little blue-eyed belle's upper-class mush mouth to street talk without a bump.

"Why, no, they don't."

"Just teach y'all napkin folding and thank-you note writing?"

"They most certainly do not! I'm an econ major." The blonde straightened her back and jiggled her shoulders. "And I don't know why you're being so mean. Acting like you went to public school or something. I just asked you about Chill. I don't know why you're so upset."

But whatever Laura had stuck in her craw, she wasn't giving it up so easily.

"They teach you other stuff when you take your field trips over to the Squeeze?"

Her tone was light, as innocent as cotton candy.

Sam jerked and almost dropped her Perrier atop the discarded cheese puff. *Incredible.* Here she was lurking on deb types on the off chance she'd pick up some skinny about the joint on Peachtree at Tenth, and this pretty thing just fired its name like a bullet. She couldn't believe her luck.

"I don't know what you're talking about."

"Uh-huh. I bet you do."

"I do not."

"Get real, Miranda. I know all about you."

"You do *not!*"

With that, Miranda, finally realizing she'd bitten off more than she could chew, stomped away, flouncing the pink skirt of her party dress, just exactly the same shade, Sam bet, she'd worn when she was four. Showing a very neat little pair of legs.

Certainly neat enough to shake up the dirty old men who were paying for peep shows and perhaps other kinds of extracurriculars staged by young girls of a certain station over at the Tight Squeeze.

Sam hadn't been able to get the tip off her mind, the one her plainclothes friend Charlie had handed her over a beer last week. *His* beer. She'd been off the sauce for almost a decade.

"Funny, ain't it?" he'd asked, sliding an eye for the thousandth time over a badly painted nude hanging in Manuel's front room. Sam's favorite hangout was an old-fashioned place known for its camaraderie rather than its interior decoration.

"What?"

"I was just thinking, for all of its Bible-thumping, Atlanta's one of the few places in the country where it's legal for strippers to fraternize. Peel all the pretties off and shake it right in a man's face."

"What the hell are you talking about?"

"Strip joints."

"And why to me?"

"Hold your horses." He took a long sip of beer. "Now about these strippers."

Sam couldn't hold them. "You think this ace investigative reporter gives a damn about peelers? Ecdysiasts? *Stripteuse?*" She leaned back in the booth and dragged that last one out through her elegant nose, then slurped up another oyster.

"You punch the button on your thesaurus?"

"Uh-huh."

"But you didn't say the magic words."

"So?"

He reached under his badge and ID for his pen, then grabbed one of Manuel's napkins. Charlie had a flair for the melodramatic, spent his nights off playing in amateur Gilbert and Sullivan productions. Sam had caught his not-bad baritone in *H.M.S. Pinafore,* which is why he said he kept doing her favors—so she wouldn't tattle on his secret life. The truth was, she'd cozied up to and disarmed a shooter in a shopping-center parking lot the second week after she'd moved back to Atlanta and, in the process, saved Charlie's life. It wasn't the sort of thing that slipped his mind.

She'd turned the napkin around. "I can't read your writing."

"Society strippers." He said it louder than he meant to, and a passing waiter shot them a look that Sam ricocheted back at Charlie.

"What the hell are you talking about?"

"You're repeating yourself. Sure you don't want another soda? No? Well, I'm talking about little girls in special, live-and-in-color performances over at Tight Squeeze, the strip hole. Talking doing the hootchy-kootch, then sometimes joining the clientele later for private parties—if you know what I mean."

"Who and how little and why?"

"Well, we got a few from Agnes Scott—college tuition's awfully high these days. Maybe the fifteen-year-olds do it to keep themselves in crack-flavored bubble gum. Or just for kicks, little rich girls flaunting their behinds. Hell, what do I know?"

"Names?"

"Let's just say their daddies' faces, frequently pictured on the front page of your rag, are gonna be awfully red if this gets out."

"We're talking precocious girly acts and you're hinting at occasional freelance juvenile prostitution starring the cream of nubile Atlanta society?"

Of which, she reminded herself, she'd once been a part.

"That's pretty much the size of it. Photos of Vanessa Williams lost her the Miss America tiara ain't got a thing on this stuff."

"Why me? Sounds like yours. You guys too busy?"

"Sounds like a mine field blowing up is what it sounds like. Ain't nobody downtown gonna touch it with somebody else's dick."

Sam's left eyebrow lifted. "Which is why you're giving it to me?"

"Don't want to be messing with a man about his little girl."

"You think I do?"

"Sammy, love, I think these folks are right down your alley. I also think you got a natural curiosity that, no matter what, is gonna get the best of you."

So she'd opened a file and was hanging around in potted palms, which was pretty much how she worked, her deal with the paper being that if they wanted to steal her away from the San Francisco

Chronicle, it would be on her terms. She dug up her own stories, unless they had something downtown that was too tasty to pass up, and she always worked alone. She dropped into the office in the rare off-moment, skipped the whole chain of command, reporting only grudgingly to Hoke Toliver, the managing editor, whom she'd just now spotted across the Players' vestibule.

He was giving her his Jack Nicholson grin behind the back of his wife, Lois. Sam raised her glass of Perrier with her middle finger extended; he saluted her with his ginger ale. Hoke was a recovering drunk, too, the only thing they had in common, she frequently reminded him. *Except our mutual and enduring lust* was his predictable reply which she just as routinely ignored.

Suddenly there was a flurry of excitement, a drum roll, and then a burst of applause as Margaret Landry entered the room. Heads swiveled. Sam listened.

"You were wonderful, sugar."

"Child, ain't you something?"

"Lady Macbeth's got nothing on you!"

An admiring swarm circled Margaret, but then it was her theater, her performance, her party, and she was the star.

She surely looked it this opening night. She'd changed from Lady Macbeth's robes to a flowing gown of gold cloth. Her hair was a reddish halo. Margaret Landry was a short, light-skinned black woman built like a diva. Her broad face was beautiful, her smile dazzled. She beamed now at the young beauty, Laura, who had enveloped her in a big hug.

Then someone boomed, "A toast to Lady Margaret." Sam recognized the speaker. It was Mayor Andrew Young. He raised his glass and added, "To her talent."

"Her beauty," said Congressman John Lewis.

"Amen," called someone from the crowd.

"Her spirit."

"Tell it, brother," a woman added.

"And her soul," concluded former Mayor Maynard Jackson.

The power was certainly out in force tonight.

"Amen!"

Feet were stomping, gold bangles jingled. The dressed-up and sophisticated crowd was making sounds like old-time religion, having a good time.

Sam did a quick 360-degree turn around the room. Blacks outnumbered whites by about two to one, the same as the general population of New Atlanta. Not that there was anything ordinary about this crush of political and cultural movers and shakers, so elegant they glittered when they moved.

A band tucked in a corner began to play. She bounced with the music, glad to be there. Yes indeedy, she'd done right coming home.

"Ms. Adams! I am *so* delighted that you could come!"

It was Margaret Landry, the lady herself. God, the woman positively glowed.

"I wouldn't have missed it for the world. And I'm so flattered you recognize me."

"Why, *everybody* knows you. What with the fantastic work you've done in the past year, there's never going to be any hiding your light under a bushel. My dear, you're a *star!*"

Margaret's delivery had a kind of magic. A charisma that grabbed your attention and your imagination and thrilled you. She was bigger than life, a force of nature. Her very presence brought tears to your eyes.

"Why, thank you."

"Don't thank me." She reached up and tapped Sam's chin with a plump forefinger, giving her a dimple, Sam knew it. "Thank yourself."

And then, razzle-dazzle, Margaret was gone.

Oh, yes. There was no place on earth Sam would rather be at this moment. These were good times. Good people. And no matter how long she'd hidden out there in California pretending she was a sunshine girl, Southerners were her kind of folks.

She said as much to the good-looking older man who had just slipped his arm through hers, her Uncle George.

"Indeed, indeed! Couldn't agree more. Can't imagine why you ran off and left us for so long."

She flashed him a watch-your-mouth look, but he just smiled.

"You know," he went on, "I remember when Margaret Landry

first came to Atlanta, bound and determined to found her own acting group and equally set on its being the city's first multiracial theater."

"People said it couldn't be done, didn't they, George? But you helped Margaret prove them wrong." Miriam Talbot slid in and patted the arm of her neighbor and constant companion.

"Well, I didn't do all that much."

"That's what he always says," Miriam said to Sam. "But you know he used the weight of Simmons and Lee to do a lot of good. Certainly more than other attorneys I could name."

"Now, Miriam. Hold on. She's still mad at Burton Simmons for serving divorce papers on Beau," he said to Sam.

"I know."

"And what are you grinning about?" Miriam asked Sam. "I swear, between the two of you, you certainly know how to pick on an old woman."

"Old woman, hell." Sam hooted. "Besides, I can't help it. You know I think stringing up would be too good for your son Beau."

"Ladies. My dear sweet ladies," George interrupted, though he knew their bantering was all in good fun. Or *almost* all. "Samantha, how long are you going to have to be back in Atlanta before you relearn your good manners?"

"If it hasn't happened in a year, George, I wouldn't be holding my breath," Sam answered. "Besides, reporters don't have manners. Not if they're any good."

"And you are that." He rumpled her dark curls. "We need more like you spreading the good word about the South." He gestured around the room. "About successful ventures like this one."

"I think you have me confused with some other writer. Mine's the murder and mayhem beat. Remember?" Then she cocked the trigger of an imaginary pistol at Hoke Toliver as he once again passed within firing range. "Of course, this week my esteemed managing editor is trying to con me into doing some color on a bus hijacking in Savannah."

Miriam turned just in time to see Hoke waggling his ears back at Sam. "I swear, that man hasn't changed since he was a bad little boy coming over to play with Beau. Does he think that new editor brought you here to have you write about such nonsense?"

"May I warn him that you're going to put him over your knee if he doesn't shape up?"

"I might do just that." Miriam paused as a waiter approached with a tray of champagne glasses. "Here, dear." She carefully handed a tall glass to George who, mindful of his failing eyesight, took it gingerly. She turned back to Sam. "What *are* you working on these days?"

"Strippers."

"Oh. Well!"

"My dear," said George, "I'd have thought by now you'd have learned better than to ask questions like that of Sam. No more than you'd want to know the details of Beau's days."

Her son was the state's chief medical examiner.

"Oh, my goodness, no. I'd *never* ask."

"Sounds like a good plan to me, Miriam. Never does any good to ask men questions anyway." The words riffed up and down the scale.

Sam turned to find the owner of the wonderful voice, and there stood the most beautiful old woman she'd ever seen—every inch of five feet tall. Her posture was queenly, with clouds of white hair piled high like a crown. Sam straightened her shoulders.

Miriam did the honors: "Felicity Edwards Morris. Samantha Adams."

"I've heard wonderful things about you from my sister, Emily. A beautiful woman isn't long in Atlanta till word gets around."

"Considering the source of the compliment," Sam said and smiled, with a nod toward Felicity's loveliness, "I'm quite flattered." Then she couldn't resist reaching out and touching Felicity's dress. "Is this a Fortuny?"

Felicity ran a hand down the tiny pleats of fuchsia silk. "Yes, it was an antique when I bought it. A rather extreme example of the wisdom of buying good things, don't you think? Sometimes I feel like a walking museum." She tapped George's lapel. "Have you had fun reconverting this prodigal child into a belle since she's been home?"

George rolled his eyes.

"I'm afraid I'm incorrigible," said Sam. "Though I've never gotten the South out of my blood, I never was much of a lady."

"You should have known her when she was a teenager. She finagled me out of a little green sports car in lieu of a debut," said her uncle. "It hasn't gotten any better since then."

"What a delicious idea." Felicity laughed. "You modern girls! I wish I'd half your spunk."

"Why, you went off to New York when you were just a child," said Miriam.

"Oh, yes, but—well, that was very different."

Sam watched as Felicity's face clouded over. Her eyes unfocused and slid off somewhere. She began to sway, and Sam reached out, afraid that she was going to fall. But then she realized there was a rhythm to the motion, and Felicity was humming. Sam leaned closer.

"Come to momma. My sweet . . . embrace me."

The words were jumbled, though she had the right tune.

Sam turned to Miriam, but she and George had been lassoed into a conversation with a judge.

Felicity began a graceful turn. The little fuchsia pleats curved and flowed.

"Naughty baby . . . momma . . . embraceable . . ."

Sam looked around the room. Neither cops nor doctors were ever around when you needed them. Where was Beau?

"Hi, sweetie, are you having a good time?"

Sam whirled. Thank God. The ever-capable Emily Edwards was throwing her arm around her sister's shoulders.

"How are we doing here?"

Felicity shook her head, puzzled, but then her violet eyes snapped. She was on her way back.

"Aren't you proud of yourself, seeing all your hard work come to fruition tonight?" Emily continued as if Felicity hadn't missed a beat.

Felicity smiled up at her, all dimples now. The bad moment, whatever *that* was all about, was gone.

Then Miriam and George were back. "Emily," he exclaimed. "How nice to see you!"

"Yes, they let me out every once in a while."

"How are George's lessons coming?" Miriam asked.

"She means, has the Lighthouse succeeded in teaching me how to avoid making an ass of myself?"

"Well," teased Emily, "we do the best we can with the training. I make no promises about your personal behavior."

"Did you enjoy the play?" Sam asked.

"Oh, indeed," said Emily. "Of course, the Players is very special to us. Felicity does all of their voice coaching."

"I give them a little help from time to time." Felicity smiled right on cue.

"Don't be so modest," her sister insisted. "You've been a wonderful help to Margaret and the theater."

"Well, it's fun. I never had any children," she explained to Sam, "but I've always loved working with young people."

"Do you give private lessons, too?"

"Occasionally. It's hard, you know, when you get older, to do very much, but along comes a special case, young and talented, and you can't refuse. Oh, look," she said and pointed at someone behind Samantha, "there's one of my private students now."

Sam turned and followed her finger. Once again it was the lovely Laura. She was standing with her toes out now, her back against a pillar. Her tilted green eyes were locked into those of the handsome man leaning toward her.

"It's Laura Landry," Felicity said. "Margaret's daughter. Do you recognize her? She's one of the three witches in the play."

Sam laughed. A beautiful young witch was just the ticket for that silver-haired, golden-tongued devil, Beau Talbot.

My dearest Samantha, the letter had begun. Even at nineteen, Sam had been no dummy. She'd known that those three little words meant her love affair with Beau, the drop-dead handsomest intern who'd ever come down the pike, was in deep shit, for from the day she'd met him, cursing at his mother's lawnmower, he'd never called her anything but Sammy.

Her instincts were right. He went on to explain, though it was real hard to explain exactly how this had come about, his undying love for her having expired in just a matter of weeks after his having gone back to New York. Forget about their plans for her to transfer from Emory to NYU. Forget about the promise ring he'd given her. There was this girl he'd met a long time ago in Boston. He didn't know how to explain it, it was real hard to explain, but they were getting married. Tomorrow.

She'd gone straight upstairs and locked her door.

Peaches, George's housekeeper, and the only mother she'd known since she was twelve and her parents died in a plane crash near Paris, stood outside and threatened to break the door down.

After three days, Sam came out and asked Horace, Peaches's husband and the houseman and chauffeur, if he could take her bags down to the Lincoln. She'd made her reservations for San Francisco, and she imagined George could pull the strings to get her into Stanford if he tried.

She was out of here.

Love was short.

Life was long.

She was gone.

George said he wished she wouldn't, but he guessed she knew what she was doing.

He was wrong.

She didn't know diddle—except about running and hiding.

On the spur of the moment, she hid in a marriage to a bearded draft resister. After that, she pulled the covers over her head and sipped mint juleps, listening to Janis Joplin on the stereo for quite a few years. Then she got sober, got awfully good as an investigative reporter, got Sean, the chief of detectives of the SFPD, as her lover. Lost Sean a year ago to a drunk driver. Came home to George and Peaches and Horace and the grand old house on Fairview Road. Ran into Beau. And kept running into him, especially after he left his wife and moved back in across the street with his mother. He kept horning in on her stories, popping up everywhere. She told him to get lost.

"We'll set this town on its ear, Sammy. What a team we could be! Spectacular! Give us a chance."

"We're not Tracy and Hepburn here. We're not even Bruce What's-his-name and the blonde."

"Cybill Shepherd."

"She gives me gas. He needs a shave."

But maybe they were. Maybe it was kismet.

So she opened the door to her heart about half a millimeter. And her knees considerably wider. The very next evening she ran into Beau with a twenty-year-old blonde at a Braves game.

"Beau," she said and smiled and nodded at the girl.

"No!" Beau cried. "Sammy, I'm not worth your going back on the booze." She'd grabbed a beer from a passing hawker.

"I know." She smiled again and dropped it. "Excuse me," she said to the blonde. Some of the beer had splattered onto her off the top of Beau's head. "I didn't mean to hit you. By the way, this man is: a) old enough to be your father, b) a son of a bitch, and c) a heartbreaker. Git while you can, kid."

But she knew the girl wouldn't. Even full-grown women had to have the Mack truck back up and run over them several times before they got the message.

But this time Sam got it loud and clear. She had to deal with the snake professionally; after all, he was the state's chief medical examiner, and his mother was more or less engaged to her uncle. But he'd moved out of the neighborhood. She didn't want to know where. Probably a house with a round bed. Mirrors on the ceiling. A Jacuzzi, perhaps, for soothing young dancers' tired muscles. Laura, the young witch, did look like she danced.

"Sam?"

George was jiggling her elbow, nudging her back to the present and the Players' party.

"I'm sorry. Yes?"

"I was just asking you if you'd like to come over and have tea with us some afternoon," Felicity said.

"Why, yes. I'd love to."

Indeed, she would like to see more of the fabled Edwards sisters as well as the inside of their spectacular house. Yes, tea with the ladies would be grand.

Then she looked back at Laura and Beau. What did this young beauty know about Tight Squeeze?

But they were gone. Walking through that spot which they'd left, still warm, was Miranda, the blonde, Laura's companion from the side of the potted palm.

Sam grabbed Felicity's arm and pointed.

"Who's that? There. Is she one of your students, too?"

"Where? Who do you mean?" Felicity leaned, trying to be helpful, but then shook her head.

Damn.

"Do you mean the pretty blonde in pink?" asked Miriam.

Sam nodded.

"Miranda Burkett, P. C. Burkett's daughter. The deb of the year."

Sam smiled. Well. Her daddy's face certainly appeared on the front page of the *Constitution* frequently enough. So far, Charlie was right on target.

Three

"Why do you want to be running off to Fripp, for God's sakes, when you could be going to the meeting in San Francisco with me?" Hoke Toliver's hound-dog countenance was barely visible behind a cloud of cigarette smoke. He waved at a chair. "Sit down and talk."

"You know I never sit in here. Give you the jump."

"Nice talk. I should put you on report."

"Shut up, Hoke."

He grinned, stood, hitched his pants, and lit another cigarette from a burning butt.

"So why won't you come with me?"

In the past year, this had become a practiced joke.

Sam sighed, not giving it a lot. "One, I don't date men who wear crew cuts."

"I'll grow my hair."

"Not by next Saturday."

"I'll start. For you, I'll look like a hedgehog."

"Two, I don't see men in the program."

"You're in AA. What do you have against alcoholics all of a sudden?"

"It's a rule. Like not sleeping around in the office, which is reason number three."

"Not in the office. In San Francisco. In the Stanford Court." Then Hoke ran an eye around his pigsty, resting it finally on an old purple velvet sofa that a homeless copy boy had dragged in for a bed ten years previously. "Though that's not a half-bad idea."

"Four, I lived in San Francisco twelve years. I don't need to go back. Five, Lois would shoot you."

"Lois? Lois worships the ground I walk on. She wouldn't hurt the least hair on my head."

"What about what she does to your cute assistants?"

"That's none of your business."

"I need to have a talk with Lois."

"You do not, you Commie-pinko bra-burning vegetarian lesbian *Pravda*-stringer."

"I am *not* a bra burner."

Hoke leaned forward on his elbows with a loosey-goosey smile, making her aware that her green silk blouse was just a little too snug.

"No, you aren't, are you?"

She turned toward the door. "I'm not going to San Francisco, Hoke. And I'm not going to go do that stupid bus hijacking in Savannah, either. I came in here bright and early on this Monday morning to tell you I'm going to hole up for a few days at Fripp. At the beach. And that's it."

"You think because you won all those prizes and the Big Boy hired you at an annual fee bigger than a high-class hooker's—and with more perks—you can just go off and do what you want?"

She smiled. "That's the way my contract reads, boss."

"There's a story in Savannah."

"I don't do buses."

"Jesus, do I deserve this?" Hoke held his head in his hands. Sam could see his shiny skull through the short turf of his crew cut.

"It's only three or four days. Long enough to get out there, write the foreword to my friend Annie's book, and get back."

"Why can't you stay here and do it?"

"I'm gone, Hoke. In the morning."

"I want you to do the bus."

From the hall, she called, "Not up my alley."

"You are driving me nuts!" His voice trailed along behind her like a dust bunny. Then he stuck his head out of his office. Her finger was on the elevator button.

"You could do it on your way."

"Not a snowball's chance. Besides, I'm on the trail of something new. You're gonna love it." She winked. *"Very* hot."

The elevator doors closed on his strangled, "What?"

She could do a lot of her snooping from home with her modem, but to access the paper's behemoth computer, which interfaced with systems all across the country, Sam needed to come into the office. She sat now before the terminal in her office, as bare bones plain as if her name weren't on the door.

Now to see about Miranda, P.C. Burkett's blue-eyed daughter. She punched in one code after another. The screen blinked greenly at her.

She'd start with Big Daddy. Paul Coles Burkett, fifty. Listed in *Forbes* top one hundred, free-wheeling, high-born from genera-tions of rural gentry, came to the big city, bought land and started building shopping centers. Now he was developing suburban housing tracts all across the country, *then* furnishing them with shopping malls and executive parks. He'd almost single-handedly developed Gwinnett County northeast of Atlanta and one of the fastest-growing areas in the country. Needless to say, his credit rating was five stars. Sam kept checking. Burkett had five cars registered in his name: Rolls, Mercedes, Maserati, an antique Bugatti, and a Porsche. He was a member of the Piedmont Driving Club, the Cherokee Club, the Claridge, and every other social, fraternal, and professional organization that befit his stature as a major pillar of the community, the state, and the nation. She checked another file. Early in life he had listed his religious affilia-tion as Southern Baptist, but some years ago had leapfrogged to join the Episcopalians. He had contributed the limit in the past state and presidential elections, and, of course, she already knew his name was frequently bandied about as a possible candidate for public office.

Wife, Nicole Chenonceaux. As in the château. Born in Paris in 1943. Holder of a valid Georgia driver's license. The remainder of her statistics—property, credit, etc.—tied in with her husband's. Nicole Burkett had never filed her own taxes and was listed as her husband's dependent. Sam tried a few more files. Nothing more seemed to be available. Interesting. Money certainly could buy privacy.

Children. Miranda, nineteen. Ah-ha. Sam punched in another code. No arrests. Well, did she really expect the mega-developer's daughter to have a sheet? The holder of several gold and one platinum credit card in her own name. Charge accounts at all the right stores in Atlanta and several in New York. She'd spent a couple of years at boarding school in Switzerland. That was mighty tall cotton even for Georgia society. Presently a freshman at Agnes Scott. So, they'd brought the young lady back home. And that was all the dope she could scare up on Miranda.

One son, Paul, Jr., fifteen. A sophomore at Westminister. A soccer star.

Burkett's ancestral home, Belle Meade, white columned, no doubt, was down south near Waycross. Here in town, the Burketts lived on Habersham Road, out by the governor's mansion with the rest of the old money. A co-op on Park Avenue. A house in Paris.

P.C.'s various business holdings went on for years. Some private, some corporate. Lots of land. Some Texas oil holdings. Some Manhattan properties. A small island in the Caribbean.

Nothing that she hadn't expected. Except Miranda's mother being French, that was sort of interesting. Southern gentlemen, especially very rich and powerful ones, usually treated marriage as a merger, plumping up the bloodlines and the landholdings close to home. But it looked like P.C. was his own man in affairs of the heart.

Why was there nothing in the system about Nicole, though? Curious. Sam tried Nicole's name again several ways. Nothing. No record of schooling. No previous marriages. Zipola. She'd have to dig up the code book for Paris records.

But back to the main event. Miranda. None of this electronic snooping had given her a clue to the question: How did the pretty little daughter of one of the nation's most rich and powerful men get her name tied in with a Tenth Street strip club? Or had she? So far Sam still only had Laura Landry's word for it—and that spoken in a fit of pique. So far, she had nothing.

"Miz Adams?"

The voice crept in through the just-cracked door. Sam jumped. It was Shirley Cahill, Squirrely Shirley, the city room office manager.

"You've been on the hookup for twenty-two minutes."

"Yes?" Sam spoke through her teeth.

"Well, you know we have to watch our pennies these days. So did you set your timer when you punched on?"

The Squirrel wasn't giving up. Sam knew she was playing to an audience in the room behind her. The fat-cheeked woman had been put up to this by other editors, Sam's independence having not exactly bought her a lot of friends on staff.

"I'm not boiling an egg in here, Shirl."

"I know, but you're supposed to set your timer. Didn't you read the memo? You only get fifteen minutes at a time on the big system, unless you've got written permission." There was giggling from the city room.

"I'm a grownup, Shirl. I don't bring notes from home."

"But—"

"But squat." Sam was advancing now, backing Shirl out the door. "Get out of my way or I'll break your glasses."

Shirley jumped.

Then Sam smiled her sweetest as she trooped past her. The small knot of giggling reporters scattered, stepping on one another's toes.

Then Sam stopped and patted Shirley's bony shoulder. The woman recoiled. "Hell, I was only kidding," Sam said. "I wouldn't touch your glasses for a million dollars. Never forgive myself if something happened to those rhinestones."

Shirley raised her hand to the frames she'd been ever so careful with since high school.

Sam marched through the city room. She'd come back later when fewer of the troops were around and Shirl was home clipping laundry detergent coupons. Then she'd see what she could find about the ownership of Tight Squeeze. But right now she was itching to get out there and do some live-and-in-color field patrol.

As she wheeled her silvery blue BMW out of the parking lot, she peeled a little rubber for her favorite attendant, Buster. He waved his hat like a checkered flag behind her and she was off. At the first light she checked her watch. Still an hour before her lunch date with George and Emily Edwards, who had invited them both. Plenty of time for a look-see at Tight Squeeze. If it wasn't closed. Did women rip off their clothes for money in front of strangers before lunch?

She threaded her way through heavy downtown traffic, heading toward the faster artery of Piedmont. All around her was the mushrooming campus of Georgia State, blond brick buildings wedged among the gold-domed state capitol building, a maze of marble-faced state office buildings, and the freeway. She caught the light at Auburn and glanced eastward down the main drag of the old black business neighborhood. Down a couple of blocks were the Ebenezer Baptist and the Players theater. She thought about last night, the party, Margaret Landry, her golden daughter, Laura.

Then the light changed and she made her left and zipped along busy Piedmont, heading north past the sprawling civic center to the midtown area where gays were gentrifying old three-story apartment buildings, painting the whole neighborhood pink and gray and aqua.

She found a parking place on Crescent Drive, walked the one block back to Tenth and Peachtree.

This little four-block commercial strip seemed to undergo a sea change every five minutes, and the looming presence of the brand-spanking-new IBM tower up the street was going to make even more of a difference, the few remaining small shops soon to be bulldozed for smart shopping plazas, designer coffee boutiques. But in the meantime, there it was, a marquee with three bulbs blown flashing in the clear October sunlight. *TIGHT SQUEEZE.* George had said sometime he'd tell her the history behind that name, but as she pushed open the door padded in black leatherette and the rank aroma of sour beer and stale smoke hit her, Sam's concern was the here and now.

Her eyes adjusted quickly to the darkness, a single spot focused on a young redhead whose pelvis, encased in black lace panties about the size of a glove, listlessly rotated to Satchmo's "Mack the

Knife." Her magnificent breasts would be low hangers in a few years; for now, they'd knock your eyes out. But the girl wasn't enthusiastic about her current line of work. Shoulders tucked in, head down, the scarlet mane of hair was a curtain between her and the three men who were cheerleading. Except for them, the single long room was deserted.

"Off. Off. Take it all off," one of them called.

Didn't anyone ever write new lines to use in this kind of situation?

Sam stepped closer and caught a glimpse of the dancer's face as the curtain of hair parted. She looked an awful lot like a girl Sam had heard reading at the Little Five Points Pub. Was stripping what young girl poets did now for a living? If so, Emily Dickinson would have found the eighties a tough row to hoe.

"I love you!"

Sam's glance flipped back again to the three men scrunched together at a table the size of a pack of cigarettes. Japanese businessmen already tanked up and ready for fun before the noon whistle.

"Help you?"

She turned. The man who was asking had to be a weightlifter; that is, when he wasn't collecting tattoos. The tail of a cobra disappeared up under his short sleeve. He could probably put on a hotter show than the listless girl on stage by flexing his blue-engraved biceps.

"A Perrier with lime," she said.

"A *what?*"

"Glass of soda."

"Ain't no yuppie sasparilla joint."

"Haven't heard that word since the last time I saw a western."

The bouncer/bartender smirked. She wasn't sure if he was being friendly or if he was thinking about excising her gizzard. He fingered his brown beard.

"You like westerns?" he asked.

"Uh-huh." She pointed at a table. "Mind if I sit down?"

He pulled out a chair and joined her.

"Who's your favorite?"

The music ended, and the girl slouched off stage, her G-string about a hundred dollars heavier. The tourists didn't seem to care about her lack of enthusiasm. Now their heads touched across the table as they giggled in anticipation of the next act.

"Always liked Tim McCoy, Gabby Hayes," she said. "On TV, the old Gunsmoke and Palladin."

"Partial to Lash LaRue myself."

All that black leather and whips. Sure.

Then the music picked up and a black woman who wasn't so young slid out on stage like cold molasses to the tune of Armstrong's "Why Am I So Black and Blue?"

"Great music."

"You drop in to have a glass of water and listen to the sounds or you into girls?"

First Hoke had called her sexual preferences into question, now this redneck bruiser. Maybe she'd lived in San Francisco too long. It had rubbed off.

"Neither." Sam reached in her bag for the card she'd placed on the top of a deck of possibilities.

"Cheryl Bach. *The Peachtree Ad-Visor,*" the man read aloud.

"I'm selling advertising. We're a new weekly bargain newspaper that'll be distributed free in the neighborhoods. Can give you a great rate."

"You think the yups in the burbs are interested in strippers?"

"Never can tell."

"Lady, you don't strike me as dumb, and I hope I don't look *that* stupid."

The woman on stage was doing something with her hips that presupposed being double-jointed. Or maybe triple-jointed. One of the men made a paper airplane out of a green bill and tossed it. It made a perfect hit on her left tassel. She grabbed the money, nodded a smile, and tucked it into her G-string.

"Well." Sam shrugged slowly, pretending she was embarrassed to be caught out. Always a good ploy, to let them think they'd snagged you for something little. As if you'd play it straight from then on. "I do sell advertising. But I didn't really think you'd be interested. Actually, the daughter of a friend of mine bragged that she was working here. I didn't believe her. We made a bet."

"What's her name?"

"Jackie Randolph."

It was one she always had ready in her back pocket.

"Nope."

"Pretty girl. Blonde. About sixteen."

He shook his head. "Are you kidding? Chicken like that'll get you busted."

"You ask for their birth certificates?"

"Nope. No more than I asked you for your badge."

She smiled. "I'm not a cop. Actually, I'm with the NOW patrol. I'm casing the joint before we burn it down."

It slid right off his massive back. "P.I.," he guessed again. "Private ticket. Who you looking for?"

Then they both glanced up, for one of the men had materialized beside their table, his hands neatly folded in front of his thousand-dollar suit. He bowed.

"Dance?"

He was speaking to her.

"No, thanks."

Even if she were interested, she had at least half a foot on him. He'd have planted his nose in her cleavage.

Then he pointed at the girl on stage.

"Dance?"

"*Me?* Like that? Oh, no," she said and laughed.

He bowed again and pulled an eel-skin wallet out of his jacket pocket and peeled off two hundred-dollar bills and held them out to her.

"No." She shook her head.

He added another hundred.

"You don't understand." She could feel the blood rising. She didn't look at the bouncer. She could feel the heat of his grin.

Now the fanned-out ante was five hundred.

"More than you made for ten minutes of work in your life, ain't it?" The bouncer was loving this.

The tourist was reaching into his wallet again.

Sam pushed back from the table. It was a long way to the exit sign, but that didn't stop her admirer from trailing her every step. She didn't look back to see how many bills he was waving by the time she reached the door.

"Hey, cowgirl," the bouncer called, "you want the rest of your soda water?"

Next he'd be hollering not to let the door hit her in the butt.

Four

"My dear," said George as she slipped in beside him on a stool at the Trotters bar. "I was afraid you weren't going to be able to make it."

"Sorry I'm late," she said and kissed his cheek. "I got held up by a dancer."

She turned to order her standard bottled water and lime from the white-jacketed man standing behind the massive carved bar, but he was already tucking a napkin under her glass and pouring it. "Ms. Adams," he said and nodded.

Trotters is that kind of restaurant—where, if you come three times for dinner in one year, they know your birthday, your wedding anniversary, your place of business, and your preferences in wine and drink. This is high-tech Southern hospitality, aided and abetted by a computer that sends you a birthday card and invites you in for a bottle of wine, puts you on the mailing list for the restaurant's newsletter featuring your most recent promotion. An ailing regular might be delivered his favorite meal at home or in the hospital, compliments of the management. For one international stockbroker who makes Trotters his lunch hangout, the restaurant has installed a telephone at his regular table beneath a pink-fringed lamp copied from the Orient Express. He has never been sent a phone bill.

It's smart marketing in the Buckhead neighborhood that houses, wrote *Fortune* magazine, the top encampment of business executives in the Southeast. *Buckhead*—it's uptown New Atlanta, mirror-faced office towers, a crystal-chandeliered Ritz-Carlton, art galleries, high-prep commercialism abutting Tuxedo Park, the city's richest in-town suburb filled with mansions and castles. Buckhead is rich, almost exclusively white upper crust.

Sam, one of the three women in the room, sipped her drink and surveyed the well-tailored, carefully barbered crowd. No casual eccentricity here, no Giorgio Armani linen slouch, no Miami ease. Atlanta business wears a conservative, spanky-clean uniform.

She leaned toward George's ear. "Where do they keep the cookie mold that stamps out these guys?"

George's blue eyes twinkled. "In the basement of the Buckhead Men's Shop. They send 'em out onto Peachtree all wound up and ready to go." Of course, George had always worn the prescribed haberdashery, too, but he always enjoyed a joke.

"Speaking of clothes." He stared down at Samantha's bow tie. It wasn't one of those not-quite-a-tie, not-quite-a-scarf affairs that women dressed for success wear, but a big green-and-black polka-dot one that was great with her green silk blouse, antique black tuxedo jacket, and a pencil-slim white linen skirt. "You look wonderful, my dear, but whatever are we going to do with you?"

"Feed me, for starters. I'm starving." She checked her Mickey Mouse watch with the rhinestone band. "What time is our reservation?"

"One-fifteen. Emily couldn't get away before that."

"And here she is," Sam announced.

George stood and waved in the direction Sam was pointing, though she knew he couldn't see that far. His encroaching blindness was shrinking his world day by day, inch by inch.

Emily's smile was as crisp as her tailored tan linen. "Sorry I'm late. I couldn't get out of the damned house."

"You're not. And we're delighted to see you again," said Sam. "I just got here."

"She was with a dancer," George offered.

"How lovely. Felicity champions theater, but it's dance for me. Ballet?"

Once again Sam saw the nearly naked, triple-jointed black woman on stage, the snakelike movement of her hips.

"Classical," she said and smiled.

"Well, my excuse is that one of my bitches was whelping. I

couldn't tear myself away, though I'm sure she would have been perfectly fine without me."

"Emily raises cocker spaniels," George explained, and then to Emily, "Samantha has a dog, a little white Shih Tzu named Harpo. He runs our house."

Sam laughed. "My friend Annie Tannenbaum in San Francisco used to say that if there were such a thing as reincarnation, she would come back as a Shih Tzu in a Jewish household. And then she'd turn right around and bring Harpo chopped liver from the deli."

"I know what you mean. But I breed and sell, so I try not to become too attached to the pups. It's hard, though. They are so adorable. An old maid's children."

"Some old maid," George demurred. "Emily has always been the belle of Atlanta."

"Not always, dear. I only go back to the War Between the States."

"You know what I mean. Always elusive Emily, the heart-breaker."

"I just never did seem to want to be tied down."

"Emily's like me, always on the go. We counted up one time, and between us, we'd done seventy-five countries."

"Of course, I was an army nurse for a long time. The military will help you cover a lot of territory."

"When? Ever in wartime?" Sam asked.

"Oh, yes." And then she could see memory rise in Emily's eyes behind the tortoise-shell glasses that matched the large pins that kept her white chignon in place. "I was in the Philippines, Bataan."

"Really?"

"Yes, there were nurses, too, in the camps there, held by the Japanese. Four and a half years. But," she said and shifted back to the present and the pleasant in the way that Southern ladies do, "now I just putter around with Lighthouse for the Blind."

"Putter, my foot. She's the director. The place couldn't run without her."

"Well, they're going to have to learn to. I'm phasing out now, training my replacement. But they still let me come in and flirt with the older gentlemen."

"Flirt and beat us with a stick. I never had a tougher taskmaster when I was a boy at military school."

"Well, we've got to train you right. It's bad enough that you contracted that damned disease in the Amazon. We don't want you falling down manhole covers."

"Your table is ready, Mr. Adams," the maitre d' announced. "This way, Ms. Edwards. Ms. Adams."

The horse-racing theme of the restaurant carried from the plaster jockeys outside, through the silks hung in the bar, to the prints on the walls in the Jockey Room where Emily, Sam, and George dined on tagliolini with andouille sausage, cold roasted duck with snow peas, and scallops with ginger, shallots, and mushrooms.

"The food is excelled only by the service," George complimented their waiter as he cleared and poured them coffee. They shared caramel custard and raspberries with cream for dessert.

"Now that we've stuffed ourselves like pigs at Emily's expense," George said and pushed back a little from the table, "let's talk."

"Isn't that just like a lawyer?" asked Emily. "Soften you up and then steal your eye teeth."

"Now *you* called this meeting, dear, as I remember."

"I'm only teasing. And I do appreciate your time." Then she leaned forward on her elbows and her face grew serious. "Well, I know this may sound silly, but I'm worried about Felicity, and I want to ask your advice about what to do. Now I know you don't do these kinds of favors for people anymore, George."

"I am trying to keep out of trouble."

Sam only half listened to George as he continued. She was remembering Felicity from the night before, lovely in her fuchsia Fortuny, the pleats dipping and swaying as she traveled somewhere in her own private world.

"But I also know you've always been the soul of discretion in these personal sorts of matters," Emily said.

"Tell me what's troubling you." George's bedside manner was better than most doctors'.

"You saw Felicity the other night at the theater."

"Yes," he said and nodded. "She seemed to be in wonderful spirits."

"And she is, most of the time. But she's a touch senile. She comes and goes."

"It happens to the best of us, dear. I remember thirty years ago much more clearly than I do yesterday. And I can't remember where I left my glasses five seconds ago."

"Of course." Emily smiled. "But it's more pronounced with Felicity—the swings are wider and deeper. But that's not really what I want to talk with you about. That's medical; that's *my* field. And much of that can be helped with medication if I can get her away from the clutches of the real problem."

"Which is?" Sam asked.

"Randolph Percy."

"And who might this Mr. Percy be?"

Emily described the man's good looks, his charm, his winning ways. She picked up a pack of matches and tapped the racing logo. "I think he plays the horses. And," she said and sighed, "I don't know his family."

"Now, Emily, we old fogies place too much stock on families, I think."

"I'm not an ass about that kind of thing, George. I don't mean that I want to see his pedigree. But I would feel better if I knew something more about him. He just appeared out of thin air, as it were, at one of Margaret Landry's dinner parties, and swept Felicity off her feet. He's with her practically every moment, doing his card tricks, keeping her in stitches."

"Doesn't sound bad to me," said George. "There must be more."

"Two things. Felicity has been a manic-depressive since we were girls. It's hereditary—our mother was given to moods, too. Hers is not a severe case, but she does need to take her medication, especially now that her age is complicating matters."

"And she's not?" asked Sam.

"No. Not since she started keeping company with Mr. Percy. The man not only does card tricks; he believes in all this mumbo-jumbo magic elixir business. Something he says he gets from some hot springs in California, for God's sakes." Then she caught herself. "Excuse me, Samantha, I didn't mean that all Californians are crazy."

"Please." Sam pushed away the apology.

"Does this endanger her health?" George frowned.

"Not her physical health. But emotionally she's a roller coaster."

"Hummph." George closed his eyes and grasped the bridge of his nose, thinking.

"But is she happy with him?" Sam asked.

"Deliriously. When she isn't sobbing about something that happened twenty or thirty years ago."

"You mean she slips in and out of time."

"I mean she doesn't distinguish between now and then. Sorrows from her past are as real as if they're happening now. But mostly she's happy, like you saw her the other evening."

"You said you had two concerns. What's the second?"

"I think Randolph Percy is going to try to kill Felicity for her money."

Without taking his eyes off Emily's, George raised his hand and signaled for another pot of coffee.

Five

"Well, you just never know, do you?" Sam asked, fastening her seat belt. Her car, freshly washed by the valet service at Trotters, had been waiting for them when she and George stepped out the restaurant door.

"About other people's lives? Nope. Man sitting next to you on a plane, innocuous fat man with brown shoes and short socks, could end up telling you things'd keep you awake nights for weeks. Yes indeed, lawyering and reporting—both give us license to dig around, then stand back and watch the worms crawl."

"Ever make you feel funny? Sometimes I don't *want* to know. But I do it. Suck 'em dry."

"They talk to us because we listen, Sam. People spend their whole lives talking, talking, talking with nobody paying any attention at all."

"And we do it for a living."

They were passing the High Museum. Richard Meier's white-enameled structure gleamed in the sunlight.

"Fabulous," Sam said.

"The only art museum in America that's architecture, ten, art, one."

"The furniture collection's not bad."

George snorted and Sam wheeled sharply to the right to avoid a car cutting in front of her. Peachtree was an insurance agent's nightmare, the lanes changing number and direction every other block.

"You think Emily Edwards is crazy?"

"No," George said. "Emily's one of this earth's most sensible people. I've never known Felicity all that well, though we've bumped into each other forever, but it strikes me that the two of them are like opposite sides of a coin—right brain, left brain. Responsible, flighty. Practical, creative. Science, art. Felicity's the one the crazy label would stick to if you were throwing it around."

Sam was quiet for a few blocks. Then she turned and faced George. "You think I'm going to end up going to Savannah?"

"Now why would you do that?"

"That's where Emily said Randolph Percy's from."

"So?"

"I thought we just had this conversation."

George nodded his handsome head and his silver forelock flopped. "Well, it'd make Hoke happy, wouldn't it?"

"I wouldn't be going to do that damned bus thing."

"Never say never, dear. Might pan out as the biggest story of your career."

They'd turned off Peachtree onto the wide boulevard of Ponce de Leon which was lined with once-great houses, many of them now apartment buildings. Soon they were at Fairview, their street and the southern boundary of the Druid Hills neighborhood where the old houses were still grand, as were the lawns, the trees an unbroken green canopy across the winding streets thanks to the developers in the century's early years who convinced the utility companies to run their lines in back yards.

The three-story split-timber Tudor where Sam had first come to live as a girl after her parents died was set well back from Fairview. A brick drive, reflected in many mullioned windows, wound up and then around the wide, comfortable house which was across the street from Miriam Talbot's red Georgian Revival. Now Miriam waved gaily at them from her front yard where she was poking in a flower bed.

"I want you to come over later and have some tea," George called through the open car window.

"Did you have lunch with Emily?"

He nodded.

"And there's something more you want to know. Want to pick my brain, don't you, dear?"

*   *   *

Harpo fell into a shimmy of delight the minute Sam and George opened the back door.

"Dust mop!" she cried, picking him up for a hug. His heart pounded through his strong little chest.

"We've been baking all morning long," said Peaches, coming out of the kitchen into the back hall. The pencil-thin light-skinned black woman stood with a hand on one hip—her usual pose.

"You and Harpo?" George asked.

"Sure. He's a good tester. Great nose."

"And where's Horace?"

"Upstairs at his drawing table." She hooked a thumb in that direction. "Still plotting against your bedroom."

Her husband, the family chauffeur and major-domo who was also a self-taught cabinetmaker and draftsman, was redesigning George's rooms. He was determined that by the time George went completely blind his suite would be as efficient as ship's quarters.

"The Widow Talbot's coming over to join us for some tea in a little while. You think you and Harpo could rustle us up some cookies?"

"Probably. I made about a million for my board meeting tomorrow. What you think, dog?"

"What he ought to think is that it seems ridiculous for the chairperson of the city's campaign against illiteracy to be baking cookies for its board," said Sam.

"Good thing he thinks for himself, huh, dog?"

Actually, what Harpo thought was the Peaches was going to have to play second fiddle now that his mistress was home. He followed on Sam's heels but stopped at the bottom of the wide back stairs and gave Peaches a brown-eyed apology.

"Go on, Mr. Fickle." She shooed him. "No more bearnaise sauce for you. Not in this lifetime."

In the airy yellow and white bedroom of her second-floor apartment, Sam changed into old jeans, a T-shirt, worn sneakers, then flopped on the long white linen sofa in her living room. Harpo padded in after her and collapsed on a rag rug.

"Come here, Poops." She patted a spot beside her.

He sighed but otherwise didn't move, except for his eyes which rolled up in his head and then closed.

She could do with a little nap herself. She flattened one of the bright print pillows under her head and stretched out. But when she closed her eyes, her mind wouldn't rest.

Miss Felicity in the clutches of a ladykiller? Was Emily on to something or was she nuts? Or jealous? What were the chances for romance for a septuagenarian?

If, according to statistics, her own chances as a woman near forty for finding a mate were equal to those of her being kidnapped by a terrorist, the pickings for old ladies must be mighty slim. But then, money probably changed the odds.

Yet wouldn't that be awful at any age, to think that your appeal was tied to your bank account? She herself had dated a joker or two who'd been awfully curious about her condo overlooking the Golden Gate, her expensive car, whether or not she had a private income.

But attraction was such a can of worms anyway. Who was she to say money shouldn't count? No more than a pretty face? God knows, she'd always been a sucker for one of those. After all, what had first drawn her to Sean?

She glanced at his photo on the mantelpiece. What a looker he'd been. A sharp pain grabbed her heart. Even when he lay dead in the middle of rain-slick Van Ness (she'd gotten there that quickly when she'd heard the call on the police band), he was beautiful. The impact had simply flipped him up in the air, and when he came down there was only the tiniest trickle of blood from beneath his thicket of dark red hair. His clear blue eyes were open; there'd been a little smile on his face, as if he were looking forward to something. He'd been on his way home to change. They were going dancing. That was one of the things she loved about him most, the way the man could boogie. Also, his calmness, his quiet manner, the fireworks when he did lose his temper. She provoked him sometimes just to hear him curse. There was something incredibly sexy about the fierce words rolling off his otherwise gentlemanly tongue. Those other things he did with his tongue. The fact that he thought she was the greatest thing since sliced bread. The way he made her feel protected from the world, even though he called her, in his native Brooklynese, "my tough broad." How fabulous it had been to lean on his shoulder when she tired of keeping up the facade.

She shook her head and sat up. Would she still want all that when she was Emily's and Felicity's age?

Sure. You bet.

And right now she'd like to meet this Randolph Percy. From Emily's description, he must be a real piece of work. A Southern original. They didn't make them as colorful elsewhere. At least, not that she'd met.

Nor as charming. Look at Beau. The four-flusher of all time (not to mention another pretty face), and he could charm the panties off you in half a second. Unless you kept running.

But now what about this Randolph Percy? Why would he want to *kill* Felicity? She'd asked Emily that, and she'd answered for the money. He wouldn't have to kill her for that. She'd never met a Southern lady yet, at least one of Felicity's vintage, who wouldn't just turn over everything she had to a husband. All he'd have to do was marry her.

Atlanta ladies grew up under their daddies' thumbs. They married well, sometimes with a little coaxing, and then the reins to their lives were passed on—to their charming husbands, their ever-so-charming husbands. Then the ladies spent the rest of their lives keeping themselves and their houses and their ever-so-charming children beautifully schooled, curried, and combed.

And that train of thought brought her back to the purported deb strippers at Tight Squeeze—junior members of the same milieu. What the hell were they doing? Kicking over the traces? Running little races of their own? But so safe, within the circle of their daddies' arms, that they thought they wouldn't get caught if they stepped over the line a little, occasionally took money for their favors? Or it wouldn't matter if they did. Everything would be all right, just as it always had been.

But this kind of game playing was bad news, no matter who they were. And there were prices to be paid that had nothing to do with the law. They'd learn that soon enough.

Sam knew Charlie had steered her right. She was on to something. That bouncer's eyes had slid, just a little, when she'd asked him about the imaginary sixteen-year-old. She'd poked him in the right place. She could taste it.

"Samantha!" George called from downstairs on the intercom. "Miriam's here." He paused for a beat. "And Beau."

They were all laughing as she entered the living room.

"Sammy," Beau said and stood. "How lucky I am to have stopped by just as Mom was coming over for a visit. Hope you don't mind I invited myself along."

Of course she did. She gave him a look then waved him down again to the striped sofa. She flopped into a wingback chair across the room.

"You're looking awfully pretty."

The flip of her hand said *no big deal.*

"Roses in your cheeks." He grinned. The man never gave up, though exactly what it was he wanted was still a mystery to her. Probably to him, too.

"What were you all laughing about?"

"Oh," Miriam said and fanned herself. "Beau was telling us the most preposterous story about a pig. The things my son does for a living."

"You ought to know about this, Sam. You heard on the wire about that bus hijacking in Savannah?"

"Your friend Hoke thinks it's the most important news since we pulled out of Vietnam."

Beau shrugged. "Well, anyway, it seems that the hijacking had something to do with the theft of a pig—all goes back to a feud between these two families near Savannah. The cause of the pig's death was called into question, we were asked to autopsy it."

"And?"

"Well, we don't know yet, but I'll be sure and keep you posted."

"Thanks but no thanks, though I'm sure Hoke would love to have the scoop."

"You sleep on a bed of nails last night?"

"No." I'm always this way when I see you, you son of a bitch, she thought. But given the company, she didn't say that. "Just a little harried. I've started working on something new, and I've got to take a few days and finish yet another project. I'm going over to Fripp."

"Savannah's right on your way then."

"That's exactly what Hoke said."

"Listen, why don't you let me take you to dinner tonight and tell you all about it? Might change your mind."

About what, buster?

Miriam smiled at them. She had no idea what a bounder her son was. But she must have felt something in the air as she piped up, "So, Sam, what do you think of Emily?"

"I like her. Intelligent, says what's on her mind." Sam sweetly smiled at Beau. "She must have given her suitors fits."

"She has," Miriam said. "Always one step ahead of them. One of the most no-nonsense women. You know she was in the army?"

Sam nodded. She glanced at George, who was giving her the nod to take the lead. "What about her relationship with Felicity? Maybe a tad protective?"

Just then Horace entered the room with a silver tea service and a tray of food.

"Peaches thought you might want a little bite."

"Peaches's idea of a little bite is my idea of a meal," Miriam protested.

"Praise the Lord." Beau wasn't shy, snagging a handful. "There's nothing in the world better than her pimento cheese." Then he stopped with a sandwich halfway to his mouth. "Except yours, of course, Mother."

"Don't be preposterous. I never pretended to be as good a cook as Peaches. I don't know anyone who is."

"You know she could cook for you every day," said George.

"Well, every day I can persuade her to take time out from her busy schedule."

Sam's head swiveled. What was this about? Had he popped the question?

The Mona Lisa had nothing on Miriam. "We'll talk about that some other time," she said and patted George's hand. "Now where were we? I think you asked, is Emily too protective of Felicity?"

"Somebody's always had to look after Miss Felicity," Horace offered.

"Why's that?"

" 'Cause she's no good about looking after her own self. Some women are like that. Some are sunflowers, sturdy like you all and Miss Emily. But Miss Felicity, she's a hothouse orchid. Needs a lot of looking after." Horace paused.

Plugged in as he was to the lines of communication among the retainers of Atlanta's elite, Horace had always been one of George's most valuable sources.

"She's smart enough to be on her own?" Sam asked.

"Oh, Felicity's intelligent," said Miriam. "But Emily's the one who's always run the show, since they've been living together, I mean."

"And before that?"

"Well, it was Felicity's banker husband, Joseph Morris. He and Felicity were married about forty years, maybe a little more than that. I remember they had an anniversary party at their house, and then Joseph died not too long after."

"What was he like?"

"A nice man. Responsible. Always seemed crazy about Felicity. But . . ." Miriam trailed off.

"What?"

"Well, I wouldn't say that Joseph had an awful lot of pizzazz, if you know what I mean. He was perfectly comfortable with her going off to New York for the theater or to Europe with Emily while he stayed home. Of course, that was pretty much the way it was when they met. Felicity had been to New York to live for a while and Joseph had never left Atlanta."

"Well, that was pretty daring, wasn't it? Living in New York? Going off on her own—and she must have been very young."

"She was. But it was different in those days. Girls would go to study theater and to act, which is what Felicity did. It was considered a little risqué, but acceptably so. They stayed in boarding houses that were more like college dorms with house mothers and rules and curfews. So their families knew that they were looked after as if they were away at school. Some of the houses were famous. I think Felicity stayed at Miss Agnew's."

"How long was she there?"

"I guess it was about three years."

"Two," Horace corrected.

"I'm sure you're right. You have a better memory for those things than I do."

"And her career? Did she do well?"

"Oh, yes, my dear. She was a very sought-after ingenue. Why, we would clip the notices. We were all so proud of her. We just knew that Felicity Edwards was going somewhere."

"So what happened?"

"Well." Miriam paused. "She came home. In—?" she asked and looked at Horace.

"1938. Married Mr. Morris in 1939, within six months. I remember the wedding."

"I do, too," said George. "It was the event of the season. I'd never seen so many penguin suits in my life."

"And the women, Lord. Lace and organdy that went on for years. That's when a wedding was a wedding. Parties for three months with every living detail written up in the *Journal*." Miriam laid a hand on Samantha's arm, "Dear, you would have simply died. The paper used to describe what every single lady wore and what they ate. Not your idea of journalism."

"You could gain weight from the descriptions of all those gelatin and marshmallow salads," said George.

"I can't believe you'd read a word of it," said Beau.

"Well, hell. You had to keep up with what was going on. What use was it to be the cream of Atlanta society if you didn't look for your name in the paper?"

Sam snorted. There was nothing George took less seriously than society.

"So why did Felicity leave the stage?" Beau asked. "Why did she come home?"

Miriam shrugged her shoulders. "I don't know. As I said, she enjoyed success, but it's not as if she was a *star*, don't you know? And she said that she'd had her fun and now it was time for her to get married and have children, and Atlanta was the place for that. She wouldn't want to marry some boy way up there. But she never did, I mean, she and Joseph never had children. Maybe something happened."

Horace picked up the teapot. "I'll go get some more." Sam stared at his back. He knew something he wasn't saying.

"I think Emily went up there and stayed with her for a while that last year, and then they came home. Anyway," she said and smoothed her lap, "I think I've been very patient about answering all these questions. Now it's your turn. What is this all about?"

George and Samantha exchanged a look.

"Oh, I see," she said. "Typical. You'd think I'd have learned my lesson by now."

"Now, Miriam, you know Emily did come to me as a lawyer."

"George Adams, you haven't practiced law in five years. What you have practiced is poking your nose in other people's business."

George laughed. "And romancing you."

"Fiddlesticks!" But she ran her hand along the magnificent string of pearls George had given her, Devonshire cream against her pink skin, then reached for his hand.

Beau stood, and without saying a word, grasped Sam's elbows and pulled her to her feet.

"What?"

"I think these people want to be alone," he whispered and propelled her into the entry hall. "Time for our exit."

"*Your* exit."

"Aw, Sammy. Come on."

"Out," she said and pointed.

His brow furrowed. He was even cuter when he was mad.

"Don't talk to me like I'm Harpo."

"Then go. You sneaked in here on your mother's coattails. Despicable."

"Tell me what this is all about with Felicity Edwards."

"Don't try to divert my attention. Besides, you heard what George said."

"Bullshit. Did Emily retain him?"

Sam paused.

"See? I knew it. Tell me."

"Nothing that would interest you."

"Okay." He turned. "I guess I can take a hint when I'm not wanted."

Just then, just that turn of his head, and he looked exactly like he had the night before at the party when he was talking with—

"What do you know about Laura Landry?" she blurted.

He turned back *real* slowly. She'd love to wipe that grin off his face with the back of her hand.

"Pretty, isn't she?"

"Forget I asked."

"Aw, come on." He punched her in the shoulder as if they were twelve years old. "I was only trying to get your goat. What do you want to know?"

Sam told him about the tip Charlie had given her, about the conversation she'd overheard between Laura and Miranda Burkett.

He whistled long and low. "Boy, wouldn't that be something?"

"You heard anything about it before?"

"Not a word. But then, I'm a pretty clean person, Sammy."

She let that slide. "You know Laura well enough to know if she'd be involved, too?"

Beau shook his head. "I know her mother, Margaret, a little. Beth's taken some of her children's acting classes, and she knows Laura. I guess I could ask her and see if she knows anything. Beth's pretty discreet."

"She's over at Scott?"

"Just started her freshman year."

Beau was very proud of his only child. Sam could tell he was dying for her to ask more.

"How's she doing?"

"Looks like it's going to be aces all the way. She's knocking 'em dead."

"Well, she's your daughter."

His grin almost blinded her.

"Don't let it go to your head, pal. Does Beth know Miranda, too?"

"Sure. She used to come to our house all the time when they were little. They were both at Westminister."

"You'll let me know what Beth says?"

"Over lunch."

She narrowed her eyes.

He looked at himself in the mirror and straightened his tie.

"Why do I think the answer to that particular invitation's no?"

Six

Though her neat little figure didn't tell on her, Felicity Edwards had always had a sweet tooth. It was one of life's little ironies that her sister, Emily, who never gave a damn about sugar in the first place, got the diabetes while Felicity slid through life licking honey off a spoon. Invite her to a dinner party and she'd pick at her supper, then ask if she could have two desserts and, pretty please, some hot fudge.

Given that, this scenario was no surprise.

Felicity awoke late this Tuesday morning, as was her wont, slipped out of bed and into her favorite purple quilted silk wrapper, when *bump*. At the end of her dyed-to-match purple house slipper, her left big toe hit something.

"Lordy mercy, I hope it's not a snake?" she said aloud to herself in a tremulous falsetto, her inflection rising on the end in that way Southern ladies have, as if they were always asking a question. But she was just making a little joke. The thing in her shoe was too small to be anything like that.

She shook it out.

A Gold Brick candy bar! One of her favorites!

She peeled off the gold foil wrapper and devoured the morsel of creamy milk chocolate and pecans.

There was a time when Felicity was more herself that she would have at least brushed her teeth first, but that time wasn't now. What with her substituting healthy doses of Randolph's magic elixir for the lithium her doctor had prescribed, her life had become one long ride on a roller coaster. And if along the way there was a Gold Brick or two, that was no surprise.

So when she found another *petit cadeau* at the top of the stairs, she clapped her hands in delight, then grabbed it up and popped it down.

"Oh, a treasure hunt," she cried.

She continued down the stairs, and there on the next-to-the-last step she spied a third piece of gold.

"What fun!" She picked up the pace, really getting into the spirit now, and made a quick turn through the ground floor. Nothing more in the double parlors, the dining room, the music room, the kitchen, the pantry, the utility room, the sun porch. Having completed the circle, she stood once again in the broad entry hall with her bottom lip poked out.

She stared into a massive mirror at her well-practiced pout. And then something went *ting-a-ling* in her brain and she struck a pose like one of Sargent's ladies. Her neck elongated, and the long purple housecoat became a ball gown. She relaxed the *moue* and replaced it with the faintest of smiles. From beneath languorous lids, she checked herself out. Oh, yes! She was elegant, breathtaking—and young. Absolutely like a debutante.

Then Felicity Edwards stepped out of the portrait for which she had so patiently posed, which was asking a lot of a girl with her high spirits, and walked out the front door of her parents' Elizabeth Street house. My God, what a beautiful morning! It had been a perfect year for that matter, *her* year, 1933. For Felicity was eighteen, and Atlanta was her oyster. Only a few months ago she had made her bow to society, and there was no question in anyone's mind that she was the belle of the season.

"The Depression be damned," her father, the good Dr. Edwards, had cried, pounding his fist on the table so hard his wife and the crystal shivered. "My darling daughter won't be cheated of her due because of some Goddamned fluke of Wall Street." And she wasn't.

Neither were the twenty other debs who danced with their fathers across the polished ballroom floor of the Piedmont Driving Club that spring, each and every one of them as sweet in their white net and tulle and lace as a wedding cake. And that was the point, that within a year or two the girls would be standing in a room much like this ballroom, hands joined with those of an ever-so-charming brand-new husband. For what else was a debut, this whirl of dances and parties with eminently available and desirable stag lines, culminating in Daddy's last dance, if not a wedding rehearsal?

And she had done very well. Felicity turned left now as she reached the sidewalk. Her dance card had always been filled before the band had played the first tune. In fact, she had danced so much that year that even with all the party sandwiches, the Virginia hams, the oyster and milk pies, and all those delectable desserts, her father had been afraid she was going to disappear. He had prescribed beer four times a day to keep her weight up. The alcohol had kept her head up, too, way up in the clouds so that much of the season was a hazy blur. Some nights she could hardly remember coming home to this house on Elizabeth Street, which her Grandfather Edwards had built just before the turn of the century and then later given to his son, her father, for a wedding present.

She stopped and looked back. There had never been a house in her entire life that she had liked better. Not even the townhouses of New York could hold a candle to this High Victorian Queen Anne mansion. Those were all cold stone, no matter how elegant their interiors, their public faces elbowed on either side by other buildings, pinched and cramped as if they had a headache. But this Delft blue three-story Victorian was set in a generous yard with both kitchen and flower gardens and a stable, now a garage, with servants' quarters. And a line of glorious oaks. For though most of Inman Park's trees had been sacrificed for building trench lines during Sherman's siege, Joel Hurt, the suburb's developer, had replanted oaks and exotic shrubs and trees.

Now Felicity looked up at one of Hurt's oaks that separated her home from that of the more restrained Beaux Arts house next door. Her glance swept from its wide branches down to its roots, and there she saw another golden twinkle!

She pounced on the chocolate tidbit. Oh, she hadn't had such a fine morning since—well, she couldn't remember when. She licked her fingers slowly. The chocolate had gone a bit soft in a spot of late-morning sun.

Then she crossed Euclid Avenue. There was Callan Castle, the former home of Asa Candler, the Coca-Cola king.

The Candlers had left this house some years ago and had built a much bigger mansion, Callanwolde, in Druid Hills when Inman Park had passed out of vogue. The Candlers had not only moved their house north, they had dug up their ancestors from Oakland Cemetery and taken them along to Westview. Many climbers, dragging family coffins behind them, had followed suit.

But the Edwards family had stayed put. They would never leave Inman Park, not even when the electric streetcar line stopped running downtown. They would ignore bumptious new bungalows. They would persevere through decay and decline and hang on until the neighborhood rose again with the phoenix of gentrification.

But Felicity wasn't thinking of any of that now. Felicity, who imagined herself once again eighteen, was just taking a stroll down Elizabeth Street on this bright, early fall morning.

More gold glinted beneath a hollyhock in Springdale Park and she gobbled her fourth Gold Brick.

A woman coming down the steps of her house across the street stopped and stared.

"Felicity, is that you?"

"Hello," Felicity caroled, waving the arm of her purple dressing gown. "Marjorie, have you decided where you're going away to school?"

The woman, whose name was not Marjorie, and who had finished her schooling in Virginia more years ago than she cared to remember, shook her head. If she got that dotty when she was old, she hoped they'd shoot her—just like they'd shot her favorite horse who'd broken a leg when she was at Sweet Briar.

"You better go back home and get dressed," she said.

"Oh, no. I'm all ready for Mary Eloise's ball." Felicity did a cute little turn, showing off her gown.

Bless Jesus, the woman thought, and stepped back in her house. She was late for a luncheon, but at least she could stop a minute and telephone Felicity's sister.

Felicity strolled on down the street. What luck! Right there, marching along in the grass beside her straight as little soldiers, was a parade of Gold Bricks. One by one, she picked them up. She didn't eat all these right away. Why, there were too many. She'd make herself sick. Slipped them into her pocket. Five, six, seven, eight, nine, ten . . . marching. Past a clump of golden mums that lurched out toward her. A little coarse, chrysanthemums, common like zinnias. She'd have to speak to the Restoration about replacing them. Asters would be better. Too bad they couldn't do it all in orchids. Now that would be something.

But common or not, the clump of mums was home to another Gold Brick. On the other side of the flowers, the candies marched on. They crossed Delta Place, and led her into a little triangular park.

Numbers eleven, twelve, and thirteen paved the way through the park grass. Then they stopped.

Felicity looked up.

Right in front, looking rather like a small Parisian pissoir, was an antique wrought-iron lockup box.

"A good idea," Felicity declaimed to the morning air. "Keep the bad guys fast till the police can come and get 'em." Which is exactly what the lantern-topped structure was used for in the early part of the century.

But this box wasn't locked. Its metal door hung ajar.

Felicity put a hand to it. It creaked, protesting as she pulled it wide open.

Then, "No, no, no, no!" she moaned, her cries disturbing the still-cool morning air.

For staring at her with big brown eyes was a life-size rag doll. A doll with red-brown curls, a blue-and-white-checked gingham dress, and a pair of scissors protruding from her heart. The stain around the steel was scarlet.

When Emily arrived home, Felicity was sitting in the front parlor with the rag doll on her lap, rocking.

"Oh, look," she mourned, her tears so big they seemed violet as her eyes. She held up the ruined doll.

Emily took a deep breath. She had had years of practice in being calm. She took the doll.

"Oh, dear, she's been hurt."

Felicity kept rocking, wearing that smug look on her face that Emily hated.

Drunks had that look. *I know something you don't know.* Emily didn't want to know. Keep it to yourself. But they never did. They fed you just enough to make you want to slap them.

"You said she'd be all right." Felicity rocked on. "But she isn't, is she? She's dead. Someone killed her."

"Who's the someone?"

"You wouldn't listen to me. Oh, no, Emily never listens to me. Emily's too smart."

"Felicity, where did you get the doll?"

"For me to know and you to find out." But then she changed her mind. "Where *you* left her. *You* did! I said she wouldn't be safe. But you knew better. Now look. *Now* are you happy?"

Felicity jumped out of the rocker and snatched the doll back. If Emily hadn't let go, she'd have torn it in half.

"You'd bury her somewhere and not tell me."

Outside in the kennel, one of the dogs began to howl. A shiver ran up Emily's back. It was the sound of a mother's keening.

"You'd better go see about her," Felicity said then, having shifted into perfect lucidity. "It sounds like Marilyn, doesn't it?"

It was Marilyn, the bitch who had whelped a few days earlier, nuzzling at a mouse-sized puppy who was soaked with her licking. Its brothers and sisters squirmed for position at her teats, but Marilyn ignored them. Emily picked up the limp newborn. No heartbeat. Not even the tiniest.

"Felicity, Felicity!" At the back door, Emily grabbed her keys and purse. "I'm going to Dr. Grossman's."

Felicity nodded, rocking, rocking, still rocking the rag doll cuddled once more to her breast. "Go ahead. Go on. My baby will be all right. I'll make sure of it."

She rocked and smiled and smiled and rocked. She smiled down into the doll's yarn eyes that were wide open.

Emily looked down at the puppy in her hand. Then, aping Felicity, she cuddled it to her breast. She wanted to warm it.

"Go," Felicity repeated. "Go on. Mommy understands. That's what mommies do."

Emily flew then.

Felicity kept rocking.

Seven

Oh, shit! No mistaking the flashing blue light. Sam knew the speeding ticket already had her name on it.

If only she hadn't let Peaches convince her that she needed breakfast. If she'd packed last night for Fripp instead of this morning. If she hadn't stopped by the Little Five Points Pub to ask about the busty red-headed poet. If wishes were horses, she wouldn't be so late already.

Dammit!

Harpo, who was riding shotgun, gave her a look.

Okay, okay, so she was lying.

She always drove too fast. Blame it on Horace. He'd put her behind the wheel when she was fourteen and said *go like this.* Hunkered down, elbows loose, accelerator flat out.

Don't call us when you're dead was how Peaches waved her off. The exact words she'd used for almost twenty-five years to the both of them.

"You could say *Godspeed.*"

"Leave God out of it. We'll do plenty of talking with him at your funeral."

Sam wished Peaches, who could outjaw the devil if she chose, were here now to chat up this state trooper. She watched him striding toward her in the rearview mirror.

He was wearing those sunglasses. The Canadian Mounty hat, the crisp brown gabardine uniform tailored within a quarter-inch of his behind, the slow, purposeful walk.

She shivered. The last time a lawman had stopped her like this he'd almost killed her. Murdering son of a bitch was in prison now, but he'd made quite an impression. She rubbed her wrists where he'd snapped the handcuffs on.

"License, please, ma'am."

Crap! She was still carrying California tags and a California driver's license. How many times had George warned her that she ought to get them changed? Well, it was too late now to say she was sorry.

He stared at her picture. She stared at him. He was about her age, and from what she could see around the shades, a cop from central casting. Cleft chin, strong jaw, curly brown hair, the works.

"Registration."

She handed it over.

"Now, ma'am," he said, leaning down and looking right at her, "you want to tell me about this fire?"

She shook her head.

"Well, is that little dog there dying? Are you taking him to the vet?"

"Afraid not."

"Is someone in your family critically ill? Are you racing to get to a hospital?"

"No."

"Well, then, you want to tell me why it is you're burning up the road?"

She'd been thinking of Peaches the whole time the man was talking. Horace may have gotten her into this, but her lessons at Peaches's knee would get her out.

"Well, officer," she started, taking off her own shades so he could see her big brown eyes, "I'm trying to get home." She paused and shifted her Southern accent, which came and went as the spirit moved her, into overdrive. "See, I've been living out in California a few years, and I haven't been home since I can't remember when, and I've been driving I don't know how many days since I left San Francisco, and now that I'm within a hundred miles or so of Savannah, well, it seems like I just can't wait anymore." She was hot now, flying fast and loose. "I've been so lonesome for my momma and my daddy, and my brother Rick is going to be there too. I talked to Momma last night from a *mo*tel, and she said if I got home by dinner time today, she'd have dumplings waiting on the table." She laid it on even thicker. "I know all that's not much of an excuse, but I'm sure you can understand, officer. Now you wouldn't want to ruin a Southern girl's trip back home, would you?"

There now. Scarlett O'Hara couldn't have done better.

His mouth was hanging open a little. Could they put her under the jail for lying? His ballpoint pen was still poised. He used it now to tip back his hat. She could see the line where the leather bit into his forehead.

"I'll give you credit, ma'am. It's the best one I've heard all morning."

He stepped back to his car and pulled out the crackling speakerphone. Now she could hear him calling in her license plate. She tapped her fingers on the steering wheel. Four minutes passed. The radio popped again. Mickey Mouse on her wrist now said five. Was it good news or bad that it was taking so long? Seven minutes.

Then he was back. "Well, Miz Adams, it looks like you're not wanted for any felonies in California. And your driving record looks pretty clean. What story you use on the officers out there?"

"I tell 'em the truth, just like I told you."

He laughed, but his eyes narrowed. "Listen, I'm gone let you and that little dog go this time. But I'm warning you. You got about a hundred and fifty miles between here and Savannah, and if I was you, I'd make sure I did it in no less than three hours. I reckon your momma's gonna keep them dumplings warm for you."

"I sure do appreciate that."

"Miz Adams?" He turned and threw the words back over his shoulder as he headed for his car again. "You tell such a purty story, you ever think of being a writer?"

So she was already late when she got to Savannah. Forget lunch at Mrs. Wilkes Boarding House. She didn't have time to stand in line for sixteen vegetables, biscuits, fried chicken, cream gravy, and whatever Mrs. Wilkes had today for dessert. Pecan pie. Banana pudding. Coconut cream cake. Forget it. If she were going to get to Fripp by dark, she'd have to hustle her butt to find out what she could for Emily about Randolph Percy. Then, if she had a minute left, and if she felt like it, *maybe* she'd see about that damned bus-hijacking story. Pig story. Whatever.

The address she had for Percy's home was in the historic district of this sleepy old port city, not too far from Mrs. Wilkes. She made her way down broad avenues, past crumbling brick mansions, gentrified townhouses with lacy iron balustrades reminiscent of New Orleans. The two port cities smelled similar, too, a fecund odor of ripe vegetation, hot pavement, salt water. She wheeled slowly around a live oak-lined square. This old part of town was full of squares, impediments to the free flow of traffic, but who cared? The same families had been sitting on the same porches sipping the same Madeira, fanning, chatting for centuries. No one was ever in a big hurry. Why, where would you want to go? Local thinking was, if you were in Savannah, you were already there.

It didn't take long to find the Percy house on West Gordon, looking like it had just climbed out of bed. Wisteria vines hung from loose gray brick. Flapping shutters needed paint. She shaded her eyes and stared up at the still house. Maybe nobody lived there.

Then a screen door banged, and a round-faced man with tortoise-shell glasses stepped out onto his porch at the house next door and blinked at her like a blue-eyed owl.

"You're staring at the wrong house if restoration's what you're looking for." His voice was high and weedy and a little breathless. "Tourists usually are," he raced on. "Now *this*," he said and pointed behind him, "is the result of two years of broken fingernails. *That*," he pointed back at the Percy house, "is a crying shame."

"Your house?" She meant the one he had just walked out of.

His head bobbed.

"It's lovely. You do it yourself?"

"Every brick, every board, every curl of rotten paint. Had to burn it off. *Smell?* My Lord. Makes you shudder to think what must have been in it. Ground-up bone meal."

"Awfully pretty neighborhood. Reminds me of a little of San Francisco."

His head bounced up and down again. "But this is all much older. When those boys were still living in mining camps, my house was already fifty years old. I've seen those houses," he said, pushing back a blond wave.

"It's a shame these aren't all as pretty as yours." Sam nodded at the Percy house next door.

His mouth pursed. "Nothing you can do about white trash."

He couldn't mean the Percy family. They were gentry.

"Renters there now?"

"No. The owner's still there, but I've never seen hide nor hair of anyone in two years. Just stays inside and lets the place fall down around her ears. That's trashy, don't you think?" He unfurled the newspaper he'd picked up from his front porch and glanced at the front page, which seemed to galvanize him. "Listen, I've got to run. But here." He reached in his jacket pocket and handed her a card. "That's my shop. If you want to see some *really* exquisite things, drop by. I could make you a good price."

"I'll try to do that."

The man started down the sidewalk, and then he hesitated and turned back, slightly pigeon-toed.

"How is San Francisco these days? Have you been there recently? I have lots of friends, but I've been afraid to call." His voice trailed off.

She knew he meant the Castro, the gay neighborhood.

"Quieter," she said.

"It's quieter here, too. Quieter everywhere."

"They's something, ain't they?" called the old woman working in her yard on the Percys' other side. She was wearing a tatty straw hat with holes cut in it as if for a horse. Most of the elastic had given way in the top of her orange sundress, and the woman kept hitching at it.

"Who's something?" Sam moved over to the woman's yard.

"Them gays. Well, I tell you, I heard you over there talking with him. When I was a girl it was something folks just whispered about.

It was a crime against nature is what it was. Now it's all out in the open. Well, hell, to each his own, I say." Then the woman pulled a small box out of her pocket and shook something out of it onto the back of her hand. She pinched first one nostril, then the other, snorting.

"Ain't cocaine like on the TV, that's what you're thinking. Hell, I'm too poor for that. Just an old lady's snuff. Clears my sinuses, you know what I mean?" She held out her hand. "You want some?"

"No, thanks."

"Well, what you doing nosing around here?" She leaned on her hoe and peered with hard blue eyes into Sam's. "What you looking for?"

"Tourist. Just looking at houses."

"Come on now. Tell the truth. Don't shit a shitter, what's I always say. You don't fess up, I'm gonna hit you with this hoe."

Sam jumped back and the old lady cackled. "Ha! Can't take a joke." She slapped herself in the vicinity of a thigh. "Want to come in my house and have a little snort? Ain't had a drink all day. Do me good to have a shot and a chat. Nosy young women don't come by this way often."

"I'll pass on the booze, but I'll take a glass of iced tea if you have it. Mind if we stay out here and sit on the porch?"

"Suit yourself. You're not one of them born agains, are you? Preaching at people about the evils of liquor? Trying to get their money on the TV? I hate those sons of bitches."

"Innocent on all counts."

"Ha! I didn't think so. So," her eyes drilled again, "you an alcoholic?"

Sam hesitated for half a beat. No one had ever asked her so flat out.

"Yep." She found herself nodding—almost proudly.

"Me, too. But I gave it up."

Gave up being a drunk or gave up being sober? But the old woman had disappeared into the dim house.

"Gotcha, didn't I?" She was back in three minutes, carrying two Mason jars, one filled with clear liquid and ice, one with brown.

"Made you think there for a second. Well, cheers!" She downed a healthy swig. "Ahhhhh."

"Thanks. Bottoms up."

"Now shoot." The woman settled down in an old metal chair, reaching down the front of the sundress and shifting her bosom. "What you looking for around here?"

A woman after her own heart, getting right down to it. "You know Randolph Percy?"

"Sure. That pretty boy? Known him all his life. 'Bout ten years older than he is, which means I'm old enough to do as I damned well please, and I've known him since he was a baby." She took a sip. "Always been hell with the ladies."

"Is that so?"

The woman cocked an eye at her. "Now, I reckon you already knew that 'fore you set foot on my steps. What else you want to know?"

"He ever marry any of them?"

The old lady tapped a forefinger on her nose. "That's a good question. You mean lately, don't you?"

"Whenever."

" 'Cause he was married years ago—like everybody else. Married one of them Jewish girls. You know," she said and took a big gulp, "old Jewish families are something in this town. *Buckets* of money. And just as snobby as the High Episcolopes. Neither of them'll speak to you if your family ain't been in Savannah since Button Gwinnett—he signed the Declaration, case you don't know."

"So how did that marriage work out?"

"Didn't. The Cohens, that's who he married, a Cohen about ten years older than him, my age, guess she'd given up on her chances of ever marrying one of her own. Anyway the Cohens told him after he and their daughter got back from the elopement, they didn't care if she was ruined or not, they were taking her back anyhow, and he'd just as well forget the whole thing. They were having it annulled."

"So he didn't get to keep his bride."

"Naw. But I figure he got what he wanted. Not as *much* as he

wanted. But they paid him off. A pretty penny, so I understand."
She took another sip. "That was years ago." She looked up. "You
met him?"

"No."

"Well, you ought to. You'd see why all the women flock to him
like bees to nectar. He's a silver-tongued devil, that one. Tells
women all the things they want to hear. Why he can sidle up to a
woman's plain as a mud fence and within minutes have her laughing and giggling and as pleased with herself as if she was a Savannah debutante. He's a flatterer, that one. Does magic, too. 'Course,
the best magic is making a woman think she's beautiful, but he
does more ordinary kinds, too. Pulls rabbits out of hats, flowers out
of ears. He could pull the gold out of your teeth and the diamonds
off your fingers, too, I 'magine, if you didn't keep a close eye. Yeah,
he's something, that Randolph. Yes indeedy, he knows some tricks.
Tricks between the sheets, too, I dare say."

"Now is that fact or opinion?"

"Lord! Go on with you!" The woman flapped an imaginary
apron. "You don't think I'd tell you something like that, do you?"
She paused. "Well, another drink and I might."

"He ever come back here?"

"Now and again. Brings some of his lady friends with him from
time to time, too. He still likes 'em pretty, I'll say that. And he likes
'em old. Always older than him. I swear, sometimes I say to Peter,
Peter's my parrot, I say, 'Peter, that Randolph Percy must hang
out at the Old Miss America contests.' " She cackled again in what
must have been a pretty good imitation of her parrot. "You know,
if you really want to know about Randolph Percy, you ought to talk
to his mother."

"His mother?"

"I swear. Don't make nothing like they used to. If I was the
police, I'd fire you. Miz Percy's in that house right there," she said
and pointed, "the one you was staring at. And she's been peeping
out from behind that curtain for the last fifteen minutes, getting
her eyes full."

*   *   *

"Are you one of Randy's friends?" Mrs. Percy's voice was rusty from disuse. The tiny woman was bent way over behind her screen door, her head tilted like a bird's.

"Yes'm. Name's Dana Edwin." Sam thought she'd best lay on the Southern pretty heavy. "I'm in town just for the day from Atlanta? Randolph asked me to drop by and say hello for him?"

"Well, do come in."

She followed the old lady into a front parlor where the clock had stopped in about 1929. Once-beautiful satin upholstery lay in tatters, heavy sun-bleached damask curtains were streaked with time.

"*That* Randy," said Mrs. Percy in that proud way that mothers do, as if their offsprings' slight naughtiness were just a foil to their perfection. Tapping her cane, she crept over to a dusty table and offered up a dish filled with mints that looked as if they had been around for the Great Crash. "No candy? Well, that Randy, as I was saying, is the most wonderful son. I've always been so proud of him. Don't you think he's the most clever thing?"

"Oh, yes."

"And how do you know him?"

"We met through Felicity Edwards, a mutual friend."

"He never forgets me. Not for a second. You see that?" She pointed toward a potted orchid resting atop a table inlaid with mother-of-pearl. "He sent me that a few days ago. Went to the trouble even though he's been feeling poorly. Said there was no harm in being a little early for my birthday. Now isn't that sweet?"

Interesting. Felicity grew orchids.

"I wish I could say the same for my daughter. Would you like a mint?" Mrs. Percy offered them up again, forgetting that she just had.

"No, thank you. Randolph never mentioned a sister. Now tell me, where did he learn to do all those wonderful magic tricks?"

"Doesn't surprise me." The old lady sniffed. "Dorothea was a most unpleasant child. I hate to say it about my own blood, but it's true. And she grew up to be an unpleasant adult." She pulled herself up off the loveseat and crept over to a rocking chair as if she needed to change locales to complain about her daughter, which she was obviously going to do come hell or high water.

"That's a shame."

"It is. A crying shame. But there's nothing I can do about it. She always disapproved most thoroughly of me and Randolph. Said we were too close. Silly. Mothers and sons do have a special bond. And she did have her father."

"Don't I remember Randolph saying he died young?"

"Yes. He was a coward. Killed himself. Lost all our money and then walked off the pier. Fish bait. Sheer cowardice is what it was. Poor Randolph. It was such an embarrassment to him up at school. He was at Harvard, you know."

"Hard for you and your daughter, too."

"Well, it didn't matter as much, did it? I was a woman, and Dorothea just a girl. But there was Randolph, trying to make something of himself. It was a wonder he could hold his head up."

"Well, I'm sure you're proud of him."

"Always have been. More than I can say for his sister. Dot's out in California, married herself one of those older men, I mean, he's dead now, but he was older then—and rich. She plays golf and stays tan. Ruined her complexion. Face looks like a piece of shoe leather. Newport Beach. You know where that is?"

"I do."

Sam had a friend living in that enclave of rich white Republicans who favored bright-colored slacks, Lily Pulitzer prints, and dry vodka martinis.

"She divorced us," Mrs. Percy continued.

"I beg your pardon?"

"Dot divorced me and Randy a long time ago. Said people could divorce their spouses, no reason they couldn't divorce their relatives. Just cut us dead. Haven't spoken to her in years. Just as well. She has a spiteful tongue, that girl. Spreading rumors."

"About you?"

"No. About Randy. You wouldn't believe the things—" Then she snapped her mouth shut like the clasp on a purse. She stood again, and began to inch her way out of the room.

"What kinds of things?" Sam jumped up. The old lady was escaping and she'd only begun.

But Mrs. Percy shook her head, her lips a thin line of disapproval, and kept creeping. "I'm tired. I'm going to go upstairs and take my nap now. It was nice seeing you, Miss—"

"Edwin."

"Yes. Well, give Randy my love and tell him I hope he feels better and I couldn't be happier with the orchids." And quicker than one would think possible, Mother Percy was gone.

Sam stood tapping her toe in front of the house on West Gordon. Well, hell. The afternoon had gotten hot and sticky. She hadn't accomplished as much as she wanted, and she didn't have the patience to stand in line at Mrs. Wilkes's this late. And now Harpo was glaring at her from beneath his bangs.

"Don't give me any lip, little dog. I left you in the shade of this oak," she said, untying his leash. "Not enough Spanish moss for you?"

Harpo stared at her like she was losing her grip. Well, she was. She got like that when she was near starvation.

"Come on. We can walk to the Crystal from here. Maybe they'll let you sit in the back lobby, greet your public, and suck up the air-conditioning. And I'll see if I can raise Julia on the phone."

Harpo sighed. So far this day hadn't been his dream of perfection either.

The Crystal Beer Parlor had a good deal in common with Sam's Atlanta hangout, Manuel's. Old and funky with ersatz Tiffany lamps and otherwise indifferent interior decoration, it was a watering hole for both the elite and the disaffected. The food was good and cheap and no one gave a damn how long you sat or what you were wearing. Though the hamburgers were legendary, Sam was partial to the oyster sandwich and fries.

This late in the afternoon the place was mostly empty, except for six businessmen in a long red booth who, having said the hell with the afternoon, had shed their suit jackets and were deep into beer and bullshit and peanuts.

"What'll it be, Miz Adams?" Monroe grinned down at her.

"Damn, you're good! It's been six months since I was in here."

"Twenty-five years practice."

"I ought to take you back to Atlanta with me."

"Use me on the paper?"

"Sure could."

"You want a fried oyster and an iced tea?"

"Now you're just showing off."

Monroe laughed.

"Heavy on the ice, please, sir. You seen Julia Townley lately?"

Monroe put his pen back in his snowy-white jacket. "Just missed her. She's in right before lunch with that Yankee writer's doing stories about everybody in town. Had a beer, the two of them. You need change for the phone? She's probably in her studio. You can catch her."

Fifteen minutes later Julia was sitting across from her wearing a low-cut rose-colored blouse and a cat-in-the-cream-pitcher grin. "How's tricks, darlin'?"

"Great. Fine. How 'bout you? What're you working on?"

"*Big* sculpture. Pink marble. Same color as my new lover's Johnson. In fact, piece *is* his Johnson. Wanta see?"

She dug in her satchel and handed her a photograph.

Sam kept looking at Julia's face rather than the picture.

"You're showing me this guy's dick?"

Julia laughed her huge laugh, a surprise from a woman who was five-two. But then nothing about Julia was usual.

"Look. Go on."

The man had red hair and an auburn handlebar mustache. He was built like a heavyweight boxer. Everywhere.

"Truck driver. Met him in a juke joint out on the interstate. Boy, is he something." Julia showed the tip of her pink tongue. "How's *your* love life?"

Sam shook her head.

"Girl, you better get busy. Thing rusts, it's gonna fall off."

Sam laughed, ordered another iced tea and another beer for Julia. "So what's the big news in Savannah?"

"Lord have mercy, I'll tell you what. We've been up to our *asses* in that goddamned hijacked bus."

Sam turned down the corners of her mouth.

"You know the story?"

"No. But since it seems to be my fate to hear it, I can't think of anyone's mouth I'd rather hear it from."

"Then we'll give her a shot. Grab that iced tea and settle in, honey."

Eight

"It all started a few months ago," Julia began. "No, that's not true, it actually goes back several generations to when the Tallbuttons started intermarrying, but we don't have time for that this afternoon."

"Right."

"Anyway, the Tallbuttons all live up in Bulloch County between Statesboro and Hopeulikit, about fifty miles inland from here."

"Hopeulikit?"

"Don't get hung up in the details or we'll never get anywhere. Now I don't mean to imply that we're dealing with serious incest here. These aren't the Jukes and the Kallikaks, I mean. They do use *some* discretion, hold it down to second cousins as near as I can tell, but they are all named Tallbutton, and they do all have blue eyes and red hair, though on some of them the eyes do get a bit pinkish-looking, kind of like a rabbit's, and I think they have had more than their share of albinos, but for the most part they're just plain folks, a little closer than your run of the mill, but just folks. *Crazy,* of course, but then, who isn't?"

Sam shrugged and polished off the last bite of fries, thinking about ordering some more.

"Anyway, like I said, they all live up there near Hopeulikit on a bunch of big places. Doing okay even with what the govmint has done to destroy the American farmer, they've been holding their own, keeping about chest-high out of the water, 'cause they figured out they ought to make do with what God gave 'em, and they've been growing pine trees 'stead of cutting 'em all down to clear for farmland.

"Anyway, you got these two cousins, Frank and Medford

Tallbutton, on adjoining places, and actually they been getting along pretty good for years, considering that the Tallbuttons are bad to fight. But their wives don't like each other. Frank's wife, Florence, had been known to say in public, as much as the Tallbuttons ever were *in* public, that she'd just as soon that Medford's Mavis would up and die, and it would save the Good Lord the trouble of killing her."

"I don't see the difference."

"Don't bother your pretty little head with it." Julia grinned. "Order me up another beer, okay, honey?

"Anyhow, I don't know what the original problem was between the two women. Some say it was over Florence's having given Mavis a permanent and burning off most of her hair. But anyway, they never went to the same family dos unless they had to, and then they didn't speak. Just walk around one another like the other was a broke-down armchair. But the real trouble started when Florence's and Frank's boy, Floyd, fell in love with Medford's and Mavis's Maureen."

"They all have the same initials in these families?"

"Seems like a good idea, don't you think? What with their all being named Tallbutton, it can get pretty hard to tell them apart."

"But they marry the same initials, too, it sounds like to me."

"Well, that's right, Little Miss Smarty. And if you can figure that out, you can see this match was not one made in heaven. Floyd should have been marrying his second-cousin Frankie, and Maureen was a natural for Merlin, which was what their parents had been counting on."

"How many initials do the Tallbuttons lay claim to?"

"As far as I know, they've got the Fs and the Ms and the Js and the Ts pretty well sewed up. But 'member what I said about the details."

"Not another word. Least not to you. Monroe," she said and snagged him as he passed, "another order of fries, please. No, make that onion rings."

"Not a bad idea. You're going to need it to keep up your strength."

"Should I reserve a hotel room in town?"

"Only if you're going to keep interrupting me. Now, where was I?"

"Floyd and Maureen."

"Right. So anyway, both their mothers were just fit to be tied. Here they were, hating each others' guts, and on the verge of, because the Tallbuttons are nothing if not fertile, sharing grandchildren. It was bad enough that they had to share the same county and the same name. But the plans for the wedding were moving right along, though they say that Mavis was putting the brakes on wherever she could like giving the wrong date to the woman who makes wedding cakes and forgetting to reserve the church, when Maureen up and announced that she'd changed her mind."

"Didn't want to marry?"

"Didn't want to marry Floyd. Seems as if she'd come with Floyd to Savannah to look at some veils and have their blood tests, and while they were at the health clinic doing that, she'd fallen in love with a doctor there. He looked in and saw Maureen, and they were both struck by a lightning bolt."

"Quite a step up in the world for a Tallbutton, sounds like to me."

"Well, except that he was an Indian. An India Indian, as Maureen said every time she introduced him just in case people mistook him for a Chippewa or a Cherokee. Mahatma Mehta, tall and dark with eyes like a milk cow, a welcome change for the Tallbutton genes, if you ask me. And obviously Maureen thought so. She's been heard to say she just couldn't get over how *different* he looked. But, of course, the rest of the Tallbuttons didn't feel that way. What they did was have a fit."

"Especially Floyd, I imagine."

"Well, of course. He was awfully put out. Here he was just days away from his wedding, and his bride up and jilts him for what some people might mistake for a black man. *That* I can tell you did not go down well with folks in Bulloch County, no matter which side of the Tallbutton feud they stood on.

"Of course, Florence said that Mavis had just put her Maureen up to the whole thing, that she'd never had any intention of marrying Floyd, that she'd just seduced him so she could jilt him.

"And that was tantamount to calling Maureen a whore, so that did get things rolling. But then Florence said that Maureen could marry whatever-colored person she chose to, but she hoped that she didn't think she was getting her dowry back. A bargain was a bargain, and it was no less a bargain just because she'd chosen to pull out."

"What was the dowry?"

"Well, that was the thing, see, because Florence hadn't wanted them to marry in the first place, she'd kept upping the demands. First, she said that Medford and Mavis had to give the kids a mobile home. Well, that wasn't any problem. Medford came up with a double-wide before you could say squat. Not that he wanted them to marry, either, because Mavis was against it, but once his baby daughter had made up her mind, he wasn't going to be embarrassed, nothing was too good for her. So then Florence said they needed a honeymoon, and quicker'n anything, Medford arranged for an all-expenses-paid week in Panama City. Well, Florence was fit to be tied, till she figured out what would really get Medford's and Mavis's goat, so to speak, and that was one of Mavis's pigs."

"Ah, the famous pig."

"This wasn't just any pig. Mavis had been raising prize Chester Whites for years, and they were her pride and joy. Medford used to joke that once all the kids were out of the house, Mavis was going to move the pigs in."

"And Maureen was the last kid?"

"Yep. Well, I don't know that she really would have done that, but she was crazy about her hogs. Used to nearly kill her when it was slaughtering time. And, of course, there were a couple of favorite old sows that she never did let go of—Louise and Miss Hazel."

"We're going to get to a hijacked bus in here somewhere, aren't we?"

"Patience, patience."

"I'm so sorry. Could I freshen up your beer?"

Julia nodded and Monroe delivered a cold one as if he'd been waiting.

"So anyway, Florence said that Maureen had to bring Miss Hazel with her to the marriage. She was such a prize producer, throwing a dozen at a time, that she would provide a good start for the young people."

"What exactly, might I ask, was Floyd bringing to this union?" Julia batted her big eyes. "Why, darlin', he was a *man*. What do you think he was bringing?"

That occasioned a few minutes of silly giggles.

"Cut 'em off," Monroe called to the bartender. " 'Specially the one who can't hold her iced tea."

Julia resumed. "So Florence said that was all right, Medford could cancel the honeymoon and they could sell the double-wide, but they weren't giving back the pig. Said Miss Hazel was a nonrefundable deposit on the marriage and wasn't going home just because Maureen had reneged.

"Well, of course, Mavis had a screaming hissy fit. It was one thing to be losing a daughter, but it was entirely another to be losing a favorite sow. She sent Medford over to Florence's and Frank's house carrying a double-barreled shotgun to demand Miss Hazel's return, but Medford laid it down on the porch when he got there because he really didn't intend to go shooting his cousin or his cousin's wife, even if she was, as Mavis said, a walleyed bitch."

"Meanwhile, what's happening with Maureen and Mahatma?"

"Well, Maureen didn't see any point in letting a perfectly good wedding go to waste, so they were going right ahead with it. Of course, they didn't have time to send out new invitations with Mahatma's name instead of Floyd's, but this wouldn't be the first time that ever happened. A girl in my class at school did the very same thing. And Maureen was so busy getting ready to be a bride, she didn't have time to be worrying about a pig. Besides, she always had thought her mother had paid too much attention to the livestock. And she'd never wanted the pig anyway, didn't intend to have anything to do with it, so she was just as happy things had worked out the way they had.

"By this time, of course, Mavis was beyond hissy fits, she was into apoplexy. She had just had it with all of them: Medford, who wouldn't shoot his cousin; Maureen, looking after her own self who didn't give a hoot about Miss Hazel; Florence, who'd stolen her baby; and Mahatma, who unless she was mistaken, was not only some kind of Negro but also thought pigs were unclean. Now there had never been a cleaner pig than Miss Hazel unless it was Louise. And to top it all off, Louise had taken to her sty and wouldn't get up because she just knew that they'd sent Miss Hazel off to slaughter and that she was next, no matter how many times Mavis told the sow that that wasn't true. Louise just grunted and rolled her little eyes.

"Finally, the night before the wedding, after they'd all gotten home from the rehearsal supper and had gone to bed full of fried chicken and potato salad, Mavis just couldn't stand it a minute longer. She got up and tiptoed past Medford, who was sleeping on the sofa where she'd put him when he wouldn't shoot his cousin and had left him ever since, and lit out for Florence's and Frank's house.

"There was a full moon that night, which might account for why Mavis did what she did, but anyway, she could see just as clear as daylight. She crept around the side of their barn to where Florence's and Frank's sty was, and it was full of pigs, inferior pigs, of course, and not a one answered when she called Miss Hazel's name. If Hazel was anywhere near, she would have, because she certainly knew her own name. Pigs, according to Mavis, are smarter than most dogs. Not to mention quite a few humans, though she wasn't going to name names. Well, she just took a fit on her and before she even knew what she was doing, she had set fire to their barn. It was going pretty good before they woke up, and by that time it was too late, even though Tallbuttons, who had come from all over the county for the wedding, were out in their pajamas throwing water at the blaze.

"They said Florence was cool as a cuke throughout the whole thing—that she just stood on the side with the flames reflecting off her face like Joan of Arc.

" 'Woman,' Frank couldn't help but yell, 'don't you even care if our barn burns down?'

"And she didn't even bother to respond, but you could tell she didn't care. Not a whit.

"Well, the next day everybody found out why. All the Tallbuttons in Bulloch County—which is to say, all the Tallbuttons—were gathered in the First Baptist Church of Hopeulikit to see Maureen and Mahatma joined in holy matrimony, and I'll tell you there was some buzzing going on when they got a look at Mahatma, though people were trying to be polite. That is all of the Tallbuttons except Florence. She was too busy unloading Miss Hazel out of the back of her pickup truck onto the picnic grounds that had been set up behind Mavis's and Medford's house. It was a struggle, but with the help of poor jilted Floyd, she did it. And she was standing right there beside Miss Hazel when the wedding party arrived. There was Florence, in her best Sunday-go-to-meeting dress. And there was Miss Hazel, pit-barbecued whole with an apple in her mouth."

"Oh, shit!"

"Well, I'll tell you, Mavis said a lot worse than that. And she started for Florence, but Florence was too fast. She'd made her plans well in advance.

" 'Gun it, son,' she shouted and jumped in the door of Floyd's pickup truck when he came wheeling through the yard. Those that saw it said they looked just like Bonnie and Clyde.

"Mavis left the whole wedding party behind, left Maureen and her groom—in fact, yelled at Maureen as she drove out behind Florence, 'This is all your fault. I hope you're happy now!' "

"Did Maureen cry?"

"Hell, no. Anybody who'd jilt her fiancé at the blood test wasn't gonna shed a tear over a little old thing like that.

" 'Crank 'em up, boys,' she yelled at the band, and the drinking and the dancing went on late into the night."

"Meanwhile, we've got Mavis chasing Florence and Floyd down the highway."

"Yep, and Florence and Floyd had a good little start on her, and they knew where they were headed."

"Which was?"

"Panama City. Florence had just called up and renewed those reservations that had already been made in Floyd's name. So they drove like hell into the Greyhound terminal here in Savannah, and Florence had timed it so that no sooner had they abandoned that pickup in the parking lot than they jumped right on the bus.

" 'Did you see her face?' Florence kept crowing over and over until an old man in the back of the bus yelled, 'Lady, would you shut up?'

"So she whispered, 'Did you see her face when I said, y'all come on now and have some barbecue?' Then she and Floyd liked to have died laughing.

"But that didn't last very long, because they hadn't even hit the city limits heading toward Panama City when the bus stopped at a red light and Mavis shot right through that folding door with her double-barreled shotgun. Missed the driver 'cause that's what she intended to do, but she certainly got his attention.

" 'What do you want?' he yelled.

" 'Open the goddamned door!'

"Well, you can imagine. He did. Mavis stepped on and popped right up to Florence and Floyd and said, 'You think you so smart, you got another think coming.' Then she turned to the driver. 'Drive!'

" 'No, ma'am. I can't do that.'

" 'Why not? You done lost your nerve?'

" 'No ma'am, but I can't go nowhere if you ain't got no ticket. A gun ain't the price of admission to this bus.'

" 'Hell, man, I could kill you dead.'

" 'Yep, you could. But I don't think you're gonna.'

"And he was right. Because Mavis Tallbutton may have been crazy, but she wasn't *that* crazy, so it was what we call a Mexican standoff. Except that by this time there were people out in the street who had noticed when Mavis had blasted her way through the bus door, and they had called the police who had surrounded the Greyhound like Indians around a wagon. American Indians."

"I didn't think you meant India Indians."

"I didn't." Julia grinned. "Well, Mavis hadn't gone this far to give up just like that, so she held them off as long as she could."

"How long was that?"

"A good thirty hours. Until she fell asleep."

"People must have gotten awfully cranky on that bus."

"Well, they did. It wasn't exactly a picnic. But luckily it wasn't *too* full, and it did have a bathroom. Mavis would let them go, one at a time, if they promised not to try any funny stuff. And she did let the police toss tuna fish sandwiches and canned Co-Colas in through the windows. One man was really courting disaster, though, when he said if they didn't mind, he'd prefer some pork barbecue to tuna fish."

"Uh-oh. And then eventually she fell asleep?"

"Yep. Just nodded off and the bus driver reached over and took the shotgun out of her hands and that was it. The police took her off to jail."

"So what's this about autopsying the pig? Why autopsy a barbecued pig? Didn't they eat it anyway?"

"Sure. Miss Hazel gave her all for one hell of a party. No, it wasn't that pig. I thought you didn't know this story anyway."

"I didn't. But Beau said—"

"Beau Talbot? That handsome thing! Honey, you know there are women around here have considered committing crimes just so he would come to the scene. I'd forgotten you knew him."

"We used to go out when we were kids."

"Uh-huh. And?" Julia's tongue flicked at the corner of her mouth as if licking strawberry ice cream.

"Now, Julia, I can't believe you've missed Beau Talbot in your travels."

For it was a well-known fact, well-known because she told anyone who would listen all about it, that Julia Townley had sampled most of the better manflesh that was worth bothering with in the state of Georgia.

Julia laughed her big laugh. "Honey, I've missed a few. Though I've always regretted that one."

"Well, he's right there in Atlanta. Help yourself. Now go on. Finish up about this pig."

"All right. The pig they're autopsying isn't Miss Hazel. It's one of those of Florence's that died when the barn burned down. They're trying to determine if they all died of smoke inhalation and running their heads into the walls or if Mavis had poisoned them."

"Who cares?"

"Well, the prosecutor does. They're throwing everything at Mavis but the kitchen sink. I guess they need to decide if she murdered all of Florence's pigs on purpose or accidentally, in addition to burning down the barn and shooting and hijacking the bus."

Sam finished up the last bite of her onion rings and the last swallow of her fourth iced tea and sat, grinning. "Hoke's not going to like this at all."

"Hoke Toliver?"

"You know Hoke?"

"Ummm-hummm." Julia grinned that kind of grin.

Sam reached for her wallet. "Hold it. I don't want to know about it."

"Don't you think that crew cut's cute?" Julia laughed. And then she reached over and swatted Sam with the back of her hand. "Come on, girl. Can't you take a joke? Now why isn't Hoke gonna like this story?"

"Because the big boys upstairs are going to say it's Southern Gothic nut stuff, not hard news."

"You want to tell me that all those wars and hearings and bullshit on the front page are about anything in the world except pussy and power and greed and little boys worried about the size of their dicks? What the hell do you think news *is*, girl?"

Sam dropped money on the table. "Well, you know, I never realized you were so smart, Julia. I've said the same thing more than once myself."

"Sheeeeit."

Nine

Savannah's Chief Detective Dan Clayton was blond and wiry with the kind of energy more at home in New York City than this dawdling Southern town.

He'd come around the side of his desk and was sitting with Sam, reminding her of Hoke, except instead of the cigarettes, Clayton chewed.

"Pardon," he said, pointing to his mouth. "Gave up smoking almost a year ago. Wife says I don't quit the gum soon, she's trading me in. But I do that, it'll be the rocking next," he said, the chair rocking in constant motion, "and after that the talking. She says I run races even in my sleep. But I guess you didn't come here to talk about my problems. What can I do you for? You writing about the bus kidnapping?"

"No," Sam said when Clayton finally took a breath. "Julia Townley just told me more about that than I ever need to know."

"Julia?" Clayton snorted. "She's something, idn't she? There's folks around this town think she ought to be run off, but I say, fuck 'em if they can't take a joke. Lot of high and mighty people in Savannah pretending they never screwed or went to the outhouse. You know what I mean?"

"Sure do." Then she got down to it. "You remember I called you a few days ago about Randolph Percy?"

"Oh, yes." He leaned back within a centimeter of disaster. "Now I gotcha. Well, I tell you. He's a smooth old bird. One of the slickest."

"Then there've been other inquiries?"

"Hell, yes. Had calls from departments up in Charleston, in

Macon, from down in New Orleans. One not long ago from Decatur, right next door to you."

"And?"

"It's always pretty much the same. You can't arrest a man for having an eye for rich old ladies. And I'll give it to him. He has the best taste in septuagenarian lookers I've ever seen."

Clayton was up and pacing the room now, his feet pretty much keeping time with his gum.

"The questions always come from family or friends. Never from the women themselves."

"But they're able to ask?"

"What do you mean?"

"They're alive?"

He stopped and pulled the gum out of his mouth and stared at it before popping it back.

"Sometimes, yes. Sometimes, no. Now am I right, you've got another old lady in Atlanta who's got herself involved with Percy and you're concerned about her, right?"

"Right."

"Well, I'll tell you, this is how it seems to go. Sometimes the woman dies and leaves Percy her money. Usually quite a bit of it, though I'd say he hasn't hit the pot at the end of the rainbow yet. And sometimes she doesn't die, and she and Percy have a fine old time. 'Course, I imagine she picks up all the checks, but that fact never seems to bother her. I mean, we haven't gotten any calls from *them*, complaining, if you know what I mean."

"You think he's a killer?"

Clayton turned, stared at her, and chewed for a few beats.

"Could be. Very well could be. But there's never been reason enough for pursuit."

"Any autopsies?"

"Yep, as a matter of fact. A couple. Natural causes. Complications of old age. It's not like if he does kill 'em he bashes 'em with a baseball bat. Gets kind of iffy, you know, when you're dealing with people that age. It's not the same as investigating a thirty-five-year-old who's popped off and left him a bundle. Then we'd have something to look at."

"You know the Cohens?"

"You mean the Cohen he married?"

She nodded.

"They're not going to talk with you. This was all before my time, but I know the story. Town's small enough that nothing's ever secret, and nothing's ever forgotten. I could tell you dirt from before the War Between the States if you wanted to hear it."

"Not right now."

Clayton grinned and shifted his gum.

"Didn't think so. But anyway, the Cohens paid Percy off and shipped their daughter up to an aunt in New York where she got married to Ruben Glass in less than a year. Brought him back down here with her, and they're enjoying their grandchildren in a house over to East Harris. But they all sat shiva—you know what I mean—over the marriage to Percy. Far as they're concerned, it never happened."

"So there's nobody else I oughta talk to?"

"Nobody who's gonna do you any good. What I *do* think is I wouldn't trust Randolph Percy anymore'n I'd put faith in one of those rabbits he pulls out of his hat. A snake-oil salesman if one ever drew breath. Wouldn't surprise me in the least if from time to time he doesn't help a lady along to her just reward. So if I was you, I'd get my friend the hell away from him fast as I could. Though . . ."

He stopped for a minute and stared at the wall like he saw something.

There was nothing there but a spidery crack.

"Though what?"

"Aw, I don't know." Clayton shoved his hands in his back pockets. "It's, hell, I guess it's a sexist thing to say anyhow."

"Go on. I'll hit you with my purse if it's too bad."

"That's what my wife always says. And she *does*. Except it's a briefcase. She's with the D.A.'s office, and that sucker is heavy."

"Uh-huh."

Sam shifted in her seat, enjoying him but anxious to get on with it. She'd like to make Fripp before dark.

"Well, hell, maybe it's not sexist. More likely it's just stupid. But I been thinking about Percy over the past couple of years, and sort of wondered . . . when I get old . . . I mean . . . I was a lady in my seventies and along came this snappy old dude wanted to court me and, from what I hear, make love to me, and I thought he was the greatest thing since peanut butter, I mean, if all that was true, would I really want to know he's in it just for my money?"

"What if he were in it for your life?"

Clayton shrugged. "I don't know. You think you get to a point where that's not so important either? Where you'd rather trade off a few months or a year or so of hot stuff for day after day of the soaps, watching paint dry?"

"Guess you don't know that till you're there." What a strange man. "Peculiar question for a peace officer to ask."

"Reckon the more weird you see, the more you ponder. You ought to know that."

"I do."

"So what do you think about what I said?"

"About whether it's okay or not for Randolph Percy to do in old women 'cause he gives them a few last jollies?"

"That's a raw way of putting it. No. Whether or not you'd want to go on living with nothing going on?"

"Like I said, depends how you define nothing."

Clayton stared down at her hands for a minute.

"You're not married, are you?"

Uh-oh.

"Nope. Used to be. Gave it up."

She thought about Mrs. Percy's neighbor in the orange sundress who'd said the same thing about drinking.

"You going to ask next why a good-looking woman like me isn't married?"

Clayton had a nice slow grin.

"Guess you've had this conversation before."

"Once or twice."

"So?"

"Aw, come on, Dan. You hitting on me or you about to try to fix me up?"

"Neither." He laughed. "Though being a healthy red-blooded

American male, the former has occurred to me. But since I married Pat, I've managed to keep my pants zipped up. I was a rotten son of a bitch before I met her, didn't know what the hell I wanted. Then she came along and I knew. I guess that's why when I meet a woman like you who seems to be hitting on all fours, I wonder why she's alone."

Weird. Positively strange. Men never talked like this.

He caught her look. "Forget it." He stood and walked back behind his desk, opened and closed a drawer. "I'm too nosy and I think too much. I'm sorry. It's a terrible habit."

They sat and stared at each other across his desk. Funny. She'd met him fifteen, twenty minutes ago but it felt like forever. He had that thing about him, that some people do, you knew he wasn't going to lie to you or spill your secrets. Or maybe he was. Maybe that's what made him a good cop—you trusted him whether or not you ought to.

"Sean O'Reilly, chief of detectives, SFPD," she heard herself saying. "You'd have liked him. Class-A police officer."

Clayton folded a fresh piece of gum.

"Originally from New York. He died last October."

Something tickled uncomfortably in the back of her brain. What was today? What was the date?

"Duty?"

She shook her head. "DWI. Hit and run."

"That's tough. I'm sorry." He was rocking back and forth again. "So that's why you came to Atlanta?"

"Mostly."

"You do a good job, Adams."

She looked up.

"I read your stuff. Nice job on that Dodd case. And I've seen clips on that serial case in California—the one that won you the prizes, right?"

"You're awfully flattering. I don't know what to say."

"Try thank you." He grinned. "Listen, things between your side and mine are sometimes rough. It's nice to meet a pro." He was stretching now, patting his flat belly like a fat man. "Anything I can do, anything at all, don't hesitate to call."

"I appreciate it."

"And forget all that philosophizing about Randolph Percy. Sucker's guilty of a parking ticket, we'll catch his ass. Nail it to the wall." That was more like it. *More like cop talk she was used to.*

She glanced down at Dan Clayton's desk calendar. There it was, the date she was afraid of. October fifteenth. A year ago today he died.

More like Sean.

Ten

Late all day, she was driving northward through the gathering dark, the ocean's soft breath blowing at her across the marshes. Harpo yawned in her lap, restless, ready to get where they were going.

"Long day, boy."

He licked her hand.

"Hold on. Not much farther."

She scratched his ears and he wriggled, rolled over belly up. She wondered if he remembered Sean—who'd brought him to her door, a puppy with a big red bow around his neck, a six-week-old fluff ball. Harpo was about a year old when Sean died—a year ago this very day her flame-haired lover bounced up into the air like he was showing off.

Her tears blurred headlights in the distance.

It was no mistake she didn't know what the date was. Since the first of the month she'd let the days elide. Busy, busy. Working hard. How she got through the last year. How she'd kept going.

She slipped a tape into the deck. Patsy Cline wailed—no, thank you, ma'am—she pushed eject, too close to the bone.

She tried the radio.

". . . bringing you jazz sounds through the night." The announcer's voice was blackstrap molasses, thick and dark and smooth. "Here's an old favorite—at least of mine." The man sort of hissed his Ss. "Charlie Mingus. One, two, three, four, five."

Mingus's slow-talking bass rumbled through the car as they rolled now along the main street of little old Beaufort, past big white wooden houses topped by widows' walks, turned eastward, crossed bridges and islands, or so the signs read, but who could tell? The definition between land and water blurred as the continent mushed and melded into the ocean, so different from the California coast where the mountains crashed toward the Pacific like a teenaged boy going for it, balls out, *yahoooooing* through blue air. Here the meeting was a kiss, a murmur.

On the radio a horn moaned. Seemed just the right mood for Frogmore, the tiny community of low-country blacks she was passing through. Now you see it, now you don't. A couple of stores, fried seafood spots, tar paper shacks squatting on land a developer was drooling to get his hands on to throw together some condos. The air was heavy with marsh, sea grass, and salt.

A couple more bridges. A gatehouse. Fripp. The end of the road. Her headlights flashed on George's wide-porched house. She doused them and sat in the still and the dark, not ready yet to go inside and be alone.

She probably would have sat there all night, pretending she wasn't deep in the ditch, grieving Sean, if it hadn't been for the phone.

She caught it on the fifth ring.

"Sam Adams."

"Jane Wildwood."

Where'd she heard that name?

"Little Five Points Pub. Tight Squeeze."

"You're the redheaded poet."

And stripper. Yes, indeedy. Hot damn.

"Heard you're looking for me."

"Wouldn't mind having a chat."

A plume of smoke shooshed out on the other end of the line.

"So talk."

"Saw you the other day at Tight Squeeze."

"Uh-huh."

Sam would have sworn she could hear gum shift in the girl's mouth. Smoking and chewing at the same time. Dan Clayton would love her.

"Saw you, too. There and at the poetry reading. You following me?"

"Just coincidence."

"So why are you following me?"

"Really, I'm not."

"I'm not selling drugs, that's what you think. Used to hang with some guys who did, but not me."

"It's not drugs."

"Then what? You doing a story on how girl poets support themselves getting naked in public?"

"About girls getting naked in public, yes. Not necessarily poets."

"Which girls?"

"Young ones."

"Younger'n me?"

"How old are you?"

"Twenty-three."

"Oh, yeah. A lot younger."

The sound of the match striking was so close that Sam could almost smell the sulphur. Then there was a long pause.

"I don't know many girls who work there. I just do my gig and go home. Write my poetry." That last was half ironic, half a bright flag of challenge. "I do write my own stuff, you know. I've had a couple things published."

"I liked what I heard."

"Okay." Jane's voice shifted gears, getting down to business now. "What's in this for me?"

"Depends on what you know."

"I *know* what you want to know."

How hard to push her? What to offer? This was new territory. A poetical ecdysiast opened a brand-new file.

She told Jane Wildwood as much.

"Comes from *ecdysis,* casting off an outer shell."

"That's nice."

"That's what poets do for a living. Know about words." She laughed. "Words like, 'Hey, Red, you wanna fuck?' "

"Now we're getting warmer."

"I thought so." The gum popped. *Crack, crack, crack, crack.* "So,

Miz Adams. You just wanna jerk me around all night—I mean, this is costing me long distance—or you wanna get on with it?"

"Don't worry about the phone. And I'll make our conversation well worth your while. Tell me what's going down."

"That's what we're dicking around about, isn't it? What my information's worth?"

"So far I haven't heard jack."

"Jesus! Why don't you just ask me if I know anything about young society twats putting it on the line and I'll tell you yes."

Bingo. Jackpot.

"Okay, what do you want?"

"A job."

"I beg your pardon?"

The young Ms. Wildwood warmed to her subject now, shed her cool and picked up speed. "You think I want to do what I'm doing the rest of my life? I've got a degree from Florida State, journalism major, creative-writing minor. I wanna be Brenda Starr."

"You want a job at the newspaper?"

"See? You're not stupid either."

This was crazy. Who would hire this girl—with the smart mouth and the humungous tits?

Hoke.

Hoke would in a flash. And he needed an assistant. Or he would by tomorrow. He went through them like shit through a goose, hired girls for their looks, and then either they were stupid as a stone and couldn't type or they wouldn't put up with his moves. Or worse, they fell in love with him, which his wife Lois picked up on in about five seconds on the phone and fired them. Not that she had the authority, but that didn't stop her.

Little girl, if you're there in the morning, I'm gonna snatch every greasy hair off your pointed head was her favorite line. It was very effective.

Jane Wildwood wouldn't have any of those problems.

"Can you type?"

Jane snorted. "Yes, and I can spell like a son of a bitch and I know how to turn on the computer. I brush my teeth twice a day and I don't have B.O."

Hoke might even let her do a story every once in a while. Newspaper careers had started on a hell of a lot less than brains and a bitchin' body.

"I'll see what I can do. No promises."

Four beats.

"But you'll *really* try." And there was the little girl peeking out behind the tough young broad.

"Cross my heart. Now it won't be starting at the top."

"I already know about the bottom."

"Okay. So?"

"What do you already know?"

"College girls, some younger, daughters of the city's finest working out of the club."

"A private room in the back. None of it's ever open to the general public."

"They strip."

"Sure. Not very good at it. Well, every once in a while there's a talented amateur."

"And sometimes they go home with the clientele when the show's over."

Jane laughed. "Sure do. Shocking, isn't it?"

Sam knew when she was being put on.

"Technically prostitution."

"Make a big splash on the front page for you."

"Who owns the place?"

Silence.

"Can you give me some girls' names?"

Nothing.

"What's happening here, Jane?"

"Nothing, seems to me. You're doing all the taking, me the giving. Already done all of that I plan to in my young life. Ready to build up some stash on *my* side of the line."

"I told you I'll do what I can."

"I'd like to see some proof of that."

"I've got a book intro to write for a friend here. This is Tuesday —be back Friday, Saturday at the latest. Take care of you then."

"Uh-huh."

She was shut down.

"I'm not putting you on. I'll do it."

"In two, three days, you'll probably have me arrested, run out of town on some bullshit charges."

"For what?"

"Who knows? I know how you rich bitches work. Get what you want and give me the shaft."

This girl had been around the block more than once. Sam wasn't sure she *ever* wanted to see her résumé.

"When's soon enough for you?"

"Tomorrow."

"Jesus, what difference does a couple of days make?"

"Tomorrow or forget it."

"I *said* I'll help you. You have my word."

"Tomorrow."

"Your record's stuck."

"Okay, Wednesday."

"That's tomorrow. God almighty. This is really not negotiable?"

"Nope."

"And if I come in tomorrow and do what I can at the paper—"

"Take me to the paper," Jane interrupted.

"Christ. *Take* you to the paper, you'll give me names of girls and the owners?"

"Yep."

"You know Miranda Burkett?"

Jane laughed again, slyly this time. Had her where she wanted her, didn't she? No doubt about it.

"Might. Just might."

She couldn't wait for Jane Wildwood to get her hands on Hoke. She'd take no prisoners.

As Sam drifted off to sleep that night, just before she fell over the edge, she saw Sean's face, handsome, wet with rain, lying there in the middle of Van Ness Avenue. She knew she hadn't really let Jane Wildwood bamboozle her. She'd been looking for an excuse, any reason, to get back home and away from herself and her memories of that night a year ago. She didn't really want to stay anywhere by herself. Certainly not within easy reaching distance of a bottle of vodka. Jane Wildwood had good luck and great timing.

Eleven

Sam had barely pulled her car in beside George's black Lincoln early the next afternoon when Peaches hailed her out the back door.

"What're you doing home?" Then, in the next breath, she said, "I've got Miss Emily on the phone for you. You want me to have her call you back?"

Sam took it in the kitchen.

Emily Edwards's voice was high and tight. "Samantha, I hate to bother you, but something terrible is going on. First, Felicity, and then that doll, she . . . and now he's dead."

"Slow down, Emily. Who's dead?"

"The puppy. Now I know that's not . . . but the doll . . . and Felicity's out of control . . . and . . . I just don't know."

What doll? What was she talking about? "How can I help you?"

"Oh, I know you have better things to do. I hate to be such a bother."

"You're not. Give me a few minutes, and I'll be right over."

"Would you? Oh, you're so sweet. I just didn't know . . . Felicity. . . ."

"Sit down and have a cup of tea, Emily. I'm coming."

A beaming Felicity answered the door. Wearing a long flowered dress, she looked as if she should be carrying a parasol, but instead it was a greeting card she was trailing behind her.

"Oh, Samantha! How wonderful to see you, darling. I'm so glad you dropped by."

Her voice ran scales like a pianist on speed.

"Good to see you, too, Felicity."

The old woman made no move to invite her in. She kept waltzing and twirling in the doorway. Lollygagging. Dipsydoodling with her skirt like a little girl.

Sam played along. "I love your dress."

"Oh, my!" Felicity raised one hand to her mouth, the one holding the card, and tittered. "This old thing. You like all my old clothes."

"That's because they're beautiful. What's that you've got there?"

The old woman batted her eyes. Then she leaned over and stage whispered. "A Mother's Day card."

That was interesting. Here it was the middle of October. And Felicity wasn't a mother.

"Is it an old one?"

Felicity's shock would have played to the balcony's last row.

"Oh, no! It's new. Someone just sent it to me. Just today. Isn't that sweet?"

"It certainly is. That's wonderful."

She was trying to peek beyond Felicity's shoulder. Emily had to be back there somewhere.

"Don't you condescend to *me*, young lady." Felicity had drawn herself up now, radiating indignation.

Uh-oh.

"I wasn't, Felicity. I certainly didn't mean to."

"I know about you girls." Now her tone was accusing and slithery. What this woman could do with her voice was absolutely amazing—if it didn't land on you.

"Don't think I don't know what you're up to. You and Emily."

"We're not up to anything." Sam reached out a hand and Felicity reeled away.

"Oh, yes, you are. You're in cahoots, trying to steal my baby."

With that, Felicity abandoned the doorway and stalked through the hall into the parlor. Sam followed.

"What baby?"

Felicity was leaning over a rocking chair. Suddenly she whirled and shoved a rag doll in Sam's face.

"This one!"

Sam recoiled, but quickly regained herself. So this was the doll Emily was talking about—with a big red stain in the vicinity of its heart. What fresh hell was this?

"*You* killed her!"

Felicity was really in orbit now. She'd plopped down in the rocking chair and was squeezing the bejesus out of the doll as she rocked it. With a vengeance. If it had been a real child, it would be tossing its cookies.

This was more than Sam had bargained for. Where the hell was Emily?

The back door slammed.

"Sam? Felicity?"

Thank God.

"Oh, Sam. I'm so sorry. I heard the bell, but I was out with Marilyn and the puppies."

"*You* did it! You *killed* it!" Felicity flew out of the chair and this time smacked Emily squarely in the stomach with the doll.

Emily grasped her by the shoulders.

"Felicity, sit down!"

"I will not! You can't make me! *Murderer!*"

"Sam, I'm so sorry," Emily said and turned to her, all the while gently walking Felicity backwards. "I didn't mean to get you involved in our—"

"Don't be silly."

"*You* are silly!" Felicity shrieked, plopping backwards into the chair. "*Very* silly if you think you're going to get away with this. I'll turn you in. *Murderers!*"

Though the old woman was clearly out of her head, the way she said that last word was so melodramatic that Sam had to bite the insides of her cheeks to keep from laughing.

"Do you think we killed the puppy?" she asked now, ignoring the warning shake of Emily's head.

"No goddamned puppy!" Felicity pounded the arm of the chair with her fist. "I don't give a *shit* about those puppies. Emily's! Always Emily's babies! Randolph warned me. He told me you were going to do this. You *killed* my baby." She jumped up. "I'm going with Randolph. *Today.* I'm going to pack *now*. We'll run away and have our own baby." Her chin lifted. Her mouth was determined. "You can't stop me." With her back stiff, she started toward the hall when the front door sounded. "It's Randolph. Come to take me away from here. I'll get it, thank you very much."

"No," said Emily.

Sam jumped up. "I'll get it. You stay with Fel—"

"Nobody needs to *stay* with me. I'm perfectly capable of—"

Sam, now out in the entry, threw open the door.

It wasn't Randolph.

The hall was adazzle with rainbows of light from the door's beveled glass. In the middle of all this shimmering stood Laura Landry, the golden girl.

Her skin was aglow, her eyes emeralds, her hair a brindled tortoise halo. She was an Egyptian princess dressed in tennis whites.

"Hi, I'm Laura Landry." She extended her hand. "Didn't we almost meet the other night at Mom's party?"

"Almost. Sam Adams"

"I know. I asked who you were."

Behind her, Sam heard the parlor door slide closed.

"Oh?"

"I thought you looked interesting. And *interested*—in my conversation with Miranda."

Sam pointed an imaginary gun at her head. "Got me."

"That's okay." When she smiled, Laura showed a mouthful of absolutely perfect white teeth. "I do it all the time. Actors, you know. Always studying people."

"So you'll forgive me for eavesdropping?"

"Yeah." She did a little bobble with her head. Absolutely charming. "I just found out you're *that* Sam Adams. I read the scary stories you did on that sheriff." The girl shivered.

"Yeah, well . . ."

Forget the scene in the room to your right. Adams, gather your wits, and work this conversation around to Miranda and Tight

Squeeze. It isn't every day opportunity presents itself, grinning at you, friendly as a pup.

"That was Miranda Burkett I saw you with? P. C. Burkett's daughter?"

"Uh-huh."

"I've yet to meet him."

"He's a nice man. I used to go over to their house all the time after school."

The girl was shifting from foot to foot now. Sam wasn't going to be able to hold her long.

"You and Miranda are close?"

Laura shrugged. "Well, not exactly, but you know—"

Whatever else she was going to say got lost in Felicity's wail. "Nooooooo. Noooooooooo. Leave me alone!"

Sam apologized with a flat-handed gesture. "I'm sorry not to have invited you in, but as you can—"

"I've come for my lesson. Felicity's my voice coach. Is something wrong with her?"

Now she was trying to see into the house past Sam's shoulder.

"Felicity's having a bad day, I'm afraid. This isn't a very good—"

"Oh." Laura stepped back. She stopped with her toes in second position.

"Maybe you should come back another time."

"Okay." The girl shrugged. "Sure. I guess that's a good idea." She turned to go, then wheeled back, remembering something. "Listen, would it be okay if I came in for a glass of water? I just finished a tennis match, and I'm awfully thirsty."

"I'm sorry. Of course." Sam stepped aside.

Laura led. She looked toward the parlor, but the double doors were tightly closed. The only sound was the ticking of a grandfather clock.

"I think the kitchen's back through there." Sam pointed to a passageway behind the stairs.

"Oh, I know. I've been here a million times."

"Maybe we can talk another time."

"Sure." The look Laura threw back over her shoulder clearly

asked, *about what?* Then her long, narrow figure disappeared through the swinging door.

No doubt about it. Laura was a stunner. And so young. What was her relationship with Beau? Should she warn her about him?

None, she said to herself firmly, *of your business.* Besides, you heard her dealing with Miranda Burkett. She's no more helpless than Jane Wildwood.

They sure built girls tougher these days. Was it something in the water?

Speaking of tough, down the stairs marched Emily Edwards. With herself firmly in hand.

"I am *so* sorry, Sam. You must excuse me. I'm sure you must think me a silly old woman. I took Felicity up the back way, gave her a sedative, and put her to bed."

"Anyone would be rattled."

"Anyone might. But not Colonel Emily Edwards. It is not in my nature to be a quivering fool."

"Don't be so tough on yourself. I'm glad I was here. Now how can I help you?"

But Emily couldn't quite stop yet. "If I could survive the Japanese, you'd think I could deal with this little *contretemps.*"

Gently, she said, "That was a long time ago."

"You're right. And I *am* getting to be an old woman. I guess I just don't have the strength I used to. This business is wearing me down."

"Tell me what you want me to do."

"Come with me." Emily's grasp on her arm was firm as she led Sam toward the back door. "I want you to take this puppy for me and have it autopsied."

"Do *what,* Emily?"

"I know it sounds strange, but something crazy is going on here, and by God, I'm going to get to the bottom of it." As they walked through the house, she told Sam about Felicity finding the Gold Bricks and the doll. *"Now* this ridiculous card and my little dog. I shouldn't say it, but I think Randolph Percy has something to do with this." She stopped. "If anything else happens to my dogs, there's going to be *hell* to pay."

Sam agreed. "I'd kill anyone who hurt Harpo."

"Of course you would. Now, do you think Beau Talbot will do this if you ask him? I know it's out of the ordinary, but I do think someone maliciously murdered this puppy, and I want the best opinion on it."

"The last time I spoke with Beau, he was autopsying a pig, Emily. A puppy'll be a snap."

"You're kidding!"

"I'm not. He's right here in my purse."

Beau looked up and down the hall outside his office.

"You've got a dead puppy in your purse?"

"In a plastic bag."

"Jesus!"

"So you'll do it?"

"These laboratory facilities are state of the art, Sammy. Better than the FBI's."

"I've heard this spiel before. You took me on the tour. I saw you lift prints off bed sheets. Catch embezzlers by the lint on their copying machine screens. All the miracles of modern-day crime busting."

"I'm merely pointing out that crime lab is not here just for your convenience. Or for dealing with your friends' dead dogs."

"One dog. Singular. Belonging to a friend of your mother's." She handed him the bag. "One tiny puppy."

"Why am I doing this?"

"Because you owe me."

"I don't owe you."

"You'll owe me till death. Till they stab you with a silver stake through the heart."

"I hate it when you're like this."

She grinned. She loved it. "Listen, I've gotta run. Date with a stripper I'm fixing Hoke up with."

"What about *me?*"

"What *about* you? ASAP with the puppy, okay? I'll call you later this afternoon."

*   *   *

"Great stuff in Savannah with the bus, the pig, right? I knew you'd bring home the bacon," Hoke shot out of the side of his mouth. The other side was still on the phone. A cigarette took the middle ground.

"That's the worst pun I ever heard."

"Give us a kiss."

"I brought you something better."

"What?"

"Hurry up and finish." She turned.

"Don't you walk out of here!"

"Who's gonna stop me? Your assistant?"

"She's gone." He shrugged and added, "Lois."

Sam threw up her hands and left, closing the door just a little harder than she meant to.

"He'll be half a second," she said to Jane, who was waiting outside the door.

She was right.

"What the hell do you mean, walking out of my office like that?" He spotted Jane. "Oh, hello."

The redhead didn't wiggle a whisker.

"I walk out of your office almost every day."

"But not slamming the door," he said and smiled sweetly, anxious to change the subject. "Who's your pretty friend?"

"Jane Wildwood."

"I'm Hoke Toliver."

They shook hands.

"I know who you are."

"You do!"

Hoke's chest puffed up like a pigeon's. He *was* a pigeon.

"Like I said, Hoke, I'm not doing the Savannah story. It's not news. It's local color."

"Why, that's fine, Sam. Whatever you think. I trust your judgment. Now. To what do we owe the pleasure of your visit, Miss Wildwood?"

"I'm taking her over to Simmons and Lee. She's looking for a job."

"A job! You're a . . . ah . . . ?"

Hoke couldn't take his eyes off Jane, her short black leather skirt, and the tight white turtleneck that loved her considerable bosom.

Secretary. Sam could feel him willing Jane to say the word.

"Poet." Jane smiled. "And I dance."

"Dance!" Hoke clapped his hands together. "Isn't that wonderful?"

"She doesn't do both at the same time."

"Oh, I bet she could if she wanted to. She looks awfully talented."

"You're making an ass of yourself, Hoke."

"Would you like a job here, Miss Wildwood?"

Jane shifted her gum like the managing editor of a major metropolitan newspaper offered her a job every day.

"Doing what?"

"As my assistant. I mean, to begin with."

It was amazing how Hoke could put a fresh spin on the line each time. As if he didn't say it to all the girls.

"I'm sure you'd move up quickly. Exciting game, the newspaper business."

"She can't type."

"Good."

"She doesn't get coffee."

"Perfect."

"She doesn't speak English."

"Swell."

"You got it." Sam smiled at the girl. "Now would you excuse us for a minute, Hoke?"

"I'll be in my office when you're finished. Then you'll come on in, Jane. *Jane.*" He lifted his eyes to the heavens. "What an extraordinary name."

"He's always like that?" the redhead asked when the door closed.

"Nope. Sometimes he's worse. Just let him lick your ankle once in a while and you could end up publisher."

"I can handle it."

"Didn't doubt that for a second. Now," she said and put her hands flat on the desk, "when do I get mine?"

Jane really did have a great smile when she chose to use it. "I *do* appreciate this," she was saying while reaching into the world's largest bag. It probably held her entire wardrobe, though from what Sam had seen her wear so far, she'd need only a Baggie. Now Jane was holding out a piece of paper.

"I told you I could type."

"Only a little joke. So what's this?"

"The names and phone numbers of the girls you're looking for. And the best I can do on the owners. I think they're just fronts, though. Somebody else behind it."

"You are something, Wildwood."

"I try." She leaned back in her chair, trying unsuccessfully not to look smug.

Sam ran down the list of names. It was worse than she thought. Warren. Woodward. Delany. Graham. Teetor. MacNeil. Mitchell. Poor. Stewart. *And* Burkett. Blood ran no bluer.

Jane was watching her. "So now what?"

Sam rubbed her brow with the back of her hand and sat down. "All of a sudden I feel like I got hit with a bag of shit."

"But that's what you wanted."

"I know it's what I wanted. It's exactly what I wanted. What I was willing to cut short my trip to the beach and bring you here for. Get you this job. And now—"

And now, though Charlie had told her from the very beginning what she was going to find, she really hadn't thought about what it was going to mean when she held a list of names she'd known all her life. Add a few more and she'd have an invitation list for a party. These were the children, younger sisters of people she'd gone to school with. They'd grown up next door.

"Hmmmmm." Jane's mouth stretched tight, tucked in at the corners.

"What?"

"They didn't teach us this in school. You have an obligation to write everything you dig up?"

"Of course not. Lots of things aren't worth printing."

"And this one?"

"I don't know." Sam stood and took a little stroll around the desk while the professional in her scratched at an itch. "If I *really* wanted it bad, you could get me inside, right? Inside the action?"

"Right."

"I could get pictures with a camera hidden in my bag."

"Sure."

"I could catch the bastards with their pants down. Literally."

"Uh-huh."

"And ruin these young girls' lives."

A feature writer who'd not spoken to Sam since she'd come on staff slowed as he caught sight of Jane and then came to a complete halt.

"Hi, Sam. How's it going?"

"You're wasting your time," she said and pointed at Jane. "He's a transvestite."

"Let me ask you something." Jane leaned across the desk without a blink as the man stomped on.

"What?" She was already getting a little cranky at being asked hard questions by this girl whom she'd brought on staff only four minutes ago.

"What if the names on that list were all girls like me? From Nowhere, Florida? Grits? White trash? Would you be as hesitant about blowing the whistle? Wouldn't you just jump on the story like fresh meat?"

Sam's lips pursed to one side of her mouth and she stared off into the distance. Jane definitely had a point. Was she hesitating because of elitism? Was she toying with professional ethics because she was a snob?

"It's an interesting question."

"And the answer?"

"I don't know. I honestly don't." She ran a hand through her short dark curls. She stabbed the list with her finger. "This is gonna break their parents' hearts. But if I sit on it, not only have I compromised myself, but the crap keeps going on."

"So?"

Sam stopped pacing and leaned close in to Jane. "What any belle would do. Sleep on it. Think about it tomorrow."

"I have a suggestion. I'd call Miranda Burkett's mother."

Sam straightened. "I beg your fucking pardon."

"You know her?"

"No."

"Call her."

"Do *you* know her?"

"Sort of."

"What are you telling me?"

"This isn't part of our bargain."

"Jesus Christ, Wildwood."

"You need a quarter?"

The woman who answered the phone spoke with a French accent.

"No, Madame Burkett is not at home."

"When do you expect her?"

"Not for some time."

"Is she in Atlanta?"

"No, madame."

"Then she's away?"

"Yes, madame." But there was a little bobble there. *Sort* of away.

"Then do you mind telling me where I might reach her?"

"No, madame. You cannot reach her today."

"Is she in the country?"

"Yes, madame. She is in the country."

"In the United States of America?"

"Yes, madame."

"Excuse me for being so blunt, but *where* the hell is she?"

There was a long pause.

"I am sorry you are upset, madame. She is in Conyers, Georgia. Visiting an old friend who is there in the monastery. She cannot be disturbed."

"Conyers is only twenty miles away!"

"Yes, madame."

Another pause.

Then the woman added, "I never said otherwise."

The humorist Fran Leibowitz once wrote that the French are Germans with good food. Sam meditated on that for a minute. Then she said, "When she gets back from her *journey,* would you be so kind as to tell her that Samantha Adams called from the *Constitution* and would like to talk with her about an urgent matter?" She said her number very slowly.

"Yes, madame. To do so would be my pleasure."

Sam banged out of the empty office where she'd used the phone. Jane was settling into the desk right outside Hoke's.

"You're starting right now?"

"Don't have anything else to do. I resigned my other professional position. Where are you going?"

"Out. What's it to you?"

"Jeez! Are *you* touchy. You reach Mrs. Burkett?"

"That's why I'm going—to take a walk and chill out. The only other option is to go over and personally wring the neck of Mrs. Burkett's maid until she is dead. Do you have any other questions, Ms. Wildwood? Or would you care to tell me what you've gotten me into here?"

Jane shrugged. "Nope."

"Good."

"Except . . ."

Sam was already almost to the elevator.

"Who's this Shirley Cahill?"

Sam's grin was slow. "The office manager. Why?"

"She's all over me. Is she for real?"

"Uh-huh. But I'm sure you'll work it out."

Wildwood would eat the Squirrel for lunch. Watching the floor indicator on the elevator, Sam imagined the upcoming bout between those two. When the elevator hit the ground floor, she was already in a better mood.

From the *Constitution* offices to police headquarters was a quick five-minute walk, time enough for her to switch gears back to Randolph Percy.

"Hi, Charlie." She'd snagged him stepping out of his office.

"Haven't I told you never to bother me at work?" he growled.

A couple of uniforms gave Charlie the eye as she took his arm and he escorted her out through the headquarters lobby, which, as always, was filled with a typical sample of the city's flotsam and jetsam.

"But, darling, I couldn't get through the day without you," she said loud enough for the uniforms' ears.

"All right, all right. Enough funny business." They were on the sidewalk now. "What d'ya want?"

"Come have some coffee."

"Uh-huh. Coffee and what else?"

"You know Randolph Percy?"

"Maybe." He folded his hands over his belly. "Cost you a jelly doughnut. For starters."

The booths at Miller's Coffee Shop across the street from headquarters were exactly the same dark blue as police uniforms, both the plastic seats and the tabletops. A cop could disappear in there, which, Mrs. Miller having raised no stupid children, was the point. However, Charlie, who took the term "plainclothes" seriously, didn't meld. Miller's was actually one of the few places in town where the man in tan stood out.

Sam watched him measuring three spoonfuls of sugar and slowly stirring. He added a swirl of cream and then the coffee matched his pants and his shirt and sports jacket.

"Randolph Percy," she said.

Charlie liked to ease into things. "So you followed up on the girls at Tight Squeeze?"

"Uh-huh."

"And?"

"Just what you advertised. Big fishes' darling daughters."

Charlie pointed a finger. "You be careful. This kind of thing you can get yourself hurt."

Well, she wanted to talk about it anyway, didn't she? Here was her opener. "That's not what I'm worried about."

"Meaning?"

"I got a list, Charlie. It wouldn't take much to nail their sweet little asses to the wall."

"And you got cold feet."

She stared down at her own coffee. "Yeah."

"Well, Jesus, hon. You know I gave it to you in the first place 'cause the blues don't want to touch it. No reason *you* should bring the whole north side down on your head unless you want to."

"It's not because I'm afraid of their daddies, Charlie."

"Bullshit."

"No, really. I'm not scared of them. It's more like now that I'm into it, I'm not sure what the point is. Stripping isn't illegal. Well, maybe for minors. And going home with somebody? Hell. The more I think about it, it's just scandal. Stuff for the checkout stand rags. Not that I don't think it should stop."

"You think that because of who they are? If they were trash, would you call 'em whores?"

"Jesus! That's the same thing Jane asked me."

"Who's Jane?"

"A girl who—it's too long to explain. I'll bring her by one day. You'll love her."

"So this Jane got your dander up?"

"Yeah. She asked me if the girls weren't society, would I hesitate."

"So? Would you?"

She took a long pull on her coffee. "I think so."

She thought back to seeing Jane on that stage, her hair flopped over to hide her face. Even if she hadn't known her, would she have printed her name in the paper for having earned a few bucks horizontal? Probably not. She hoped what she'd do was try to figure out another way to bust the owners. Shut the place down.

"Why do you think they do it?" Charlie asked.

"Who?"

"The society kiddies."

"Hell, I don't know."

"Well, ask yourself, is smearing their names all over the front page going to make the situation any better?"

"It'll make them stop."

"That the only way?"

"What are you, Charlie? The good fairy or a cop?"

"That's what they call me, hon. The good fucking fairy. Listen." He put his big paw over her hand. "Just let it sit for a bit. Forget about legality. You're no virgin when it comes to that crap anyway. Let it stew. You'll do what's right." He blew on his coffee and signaled the waitress for another doughnut. "Now what does Percy have to do with this?"

"Nothing. The Percy business is something else—for a friend."

"With you, it's always something else." He wiped red jelly from his chin. "Sweet old Randy Percy, huh?"

"What've you got?"

"I call the type a Dapper Dan. Ladykiller."

"Literally?"

Like Jane Wildwood, he had an audible shrug.

"Don't know. Could be. Looks like. He's a grifter, Sammy, fancy-dressed scum."

"Been down?"

"Nah. Too slippery. He's a lawyer, you know. Those guys you can't pin anything on even with a smoking gun. It's all a game to them."

"He hasn't practiced for years."

Another shrug.

"So?"

"So, he makes money off little old ladies. Plays the horses, been mixed up with some pretty high rollers, and got pulled with some heavy bookies, but nothing that stuck. You know about the magic?" He went on when she nodded. "That crap's just for flash. Though over in Macon, he did a healing number once and raked in some bucks."

"With a magic elixir?"

"Don't confuse me with big words. Hocus-pocus. Nobody in his crowd much cares as long as he doesn't scare the horses."

"Or kill anyone."

Charlie slurped and swallowed. "Don't know that they'd care about that either. He's a slick old bird, Sammy. I wish you luck. Go home. You're looking a little tired."

He was right. It had been a long drive and a longer day. "And don't worry about that girlie business."

First thing the next morning she dug out the name and number in Decatur that Dan Clayton had given her—the woman who had complained about Randolph Percy romancing her mother. The line was busy for half an hour. Finally, she got lucky.

"Miss Finch?"

"Yes? What do you want?" The voice was whiny, already about to hang up.

Sam said who she was and why she was calling. "So I thought maybe I could come over and talk with you. I promise I won't take much of your time."

"Well, I've got to get my hair done. It's Thursday, isn't it?"

"All day."

"What?"

"Thursday, yes, it's Thursday."

"Well. My appointment's not till this afternoon. I guess I can talk with you about Mother. It doesn't matter now anyway."

"Pardon?"

"She's dead, you know."

Son of a gun.

"Oh, I'm so sorry to hear that. May I ask when she passed away?"

"Three months ago."

Just about the time he'd started with Felicity. He didn't waste time. She'd give him that.

"Miss Finch, as I said, I'm calling because a friend of mine is involved with Percy now."

"Then I don't blame you for wanting to do something. I tried. But I couldn't do a thing."

Sam didn't doubt that. Patsy Finch sounded flat, like she was out of air, almost too tired to hold up the phone. She decided to forget the face to face. She'd take what she could get on the phone.

"Sheriff Clayton said that his office had received your inquiry forwarded from Atlanta. What was it about Percy that made you call the police?"

"Wouldn't you be worried if out of the blue a man started buzz-

ing around your mother like she was sixteen years old? *And* if she
started turning over everything she owned to him?"

"I would indeed. What did the police say?"

"They said they'd look into it. But they didn't do a thing."

"Did they ever get back to you?"

"Yes. But it didn't do any good."

"What did they say? Who was the officer you talked with? Do
you remember?"

"No, but I have it here somewhere."

Sam could see Patsy Finch waving her hand around an airless
room piled with things she just couldn't get to. And never would.

"And the officer said?"

"He said that they really couldn't do anything. That Mr. Percy
hadn't committed any crime."

"Pardon my asking, but did your mother have a considerable
estate?"

Patsy sniffed. "My father left her very comfortable. He was a
wonderful businessman and was smart about insurance. He was
smart about everything. He left me some, too, of course, I'm an
only child, but the bulk was Mother's. *Then* mine."

And there was a whole other story that Sam didn't want to hear.
But something else did occur to her.

"I'm looking at a pattern here, Miss Finch—was your mother
pretty?"

"My mother? She was beautiful. Till the day she died she never
had a gray hair. People thought we were sisters." There was a long
pause. *"She* would have been the pretty sister."

Yes, ma'am. You keep talking like that, Patsy, people are going to
think you bumped her off.

Except she hadn't gotten all the money, had she? Wasn't that
right?

"Miss Finch, do you mind my asking what your mother died of?"

"Old age, the doctor said. But I'll tell you something. I got
cheated out of more than half my inheritance by that man, and I
don't think the cause was natural at all."

And there *that* was.

*   *   *

She'd barely hung up when Nicole Burkett was on the line, returning her call.

"Ms. Adams, I understand you have something of importance to discuss with me."

The lady's voice was silk, fine wine, old silver.

"Yes, I'm—"

"I know who you are. Does this concern me, or a member of my family?"

"Your family."

Madame waited. There was a polite impatience in the waiting. Not a woman to play games with, Sam guessed, unless she wanted to play for keeps.

"Your daughter. Miranda."

"Yes. I see. Can you come to me?"

"I can. When?" It was irresistible, aping the woman's crisp style.

"When is your earliest convenience?"

"Sometime later today? After four?"

"Come at six. We'll be alone. We'll have a drink." There was just the tiniest of pauses. "I'll have Perrier for you. That is your preference?"

Nothing like a woman who had the power to do some serious homework, or have someone else do it. And wasn't shy about letting you know it.

"Yes, thank you."

"And you know where I am?"

"I do."

"Till six then."

Great. By that time, she should have figured out a graceful way to break it to this lady that her daughter was taking her clothes off in public and possibly renting some moments with her sweet young body. Then she'd sit back and see what Mrs. Burkett wanted to do about it. That's what she'd figured out in her sleep, what had been on her mind when she woke up this morning. She wasn't going to do the story. She wasn't going to pursue it any further if she could find some other solution. And Jane had implied that Mrs. Paul Coles Burkett with the nonexistent past was Ms. Fix-it-all, Ms. Superwoman. Hadn't she? Well, she'd find out soon enough come six o'clock.

In the meantime, back to Mr. Percy. She punched in the code for Percy's file on her computer and scrolled through it. Review time.

That was her system. She took almost indecipherable notes like any other reporter in four-inch-wide notebooks, then input the information to her computer as soon as possible. There, with a program she'd designed, she could access, cross-index, and manipulate data in countless variations, making it stand on its head until it produced what she wanted—though, of course, she got only as good as she gave.

And she hadn't given it much on Percy.

What was his system? Where did he find these women? How did he meet them?

She punched in a code. Mrs. Percy's next-door neighbor in the orange sundress said he met them at Old Miss America pageants. Cute, but no cigar.

There now. *Emily,* a much more reliable source, said he'd met Felicity at Margaret Landry's. She'd forgotten that. The Ms. Landrys, Junior and Senior, seemed to be everywhere she turned. Perhaps Margaret could vouch for Percy and set Emily's mind at ease.

Fat chance.

Her instinct was that Randolph Percy was exactly what everyone so far, except his mother, said he was. A ladykiller. One who was playing silly games with candy bars and dolls—and not-so-funny games with Emily's dogs. Was he trying to *scare* Felicity to death? Or drive her further into madness? Why? What was the point?

Well, it was time she met Mr. Percy face to face. Maybe then she'd know the answers to some of her questions.

But first, she'd see what Margaret Landry had to say. The lady was listed, but there was no answer. No answering machine either.

Next she tried the theater downstairs. Someone at the party had mentioned that Margaret lived upstairs above the store. That's probably where she was.

"Box office," chirped a bright young voice.

"I'm trying to reach Margaret Landry."

"I'm afraid Ms. Landry is indisposed."

The child had probably learned the phrase from drawing-room comedies.

Sam identified herself. "Can you tell me where and when I might reach her?"

Four beats passed while the young woman struggled for her next line and obviously ran out of dialogue.

"She's out sick."

"I'm sorry to hear that."

"Yeah. Well, we are, too. She's been out of the show two days."

"Really?" And here she thought the show must go on. "I just called her apartment and there's no answer."

"All I know is we haven't seen her in two days, and Laura's filling in for her."

The lovely Laura understudying for Lady Macbeth—her mother's role? Interesting. The sort of thing a shrink would love.

"Could Laura help you? You want her to call you?"

She certainly wouldn't mind talking with Laura again, about Percy *and* Miranda.

"Thanks, yes, please tell her I called."

The Burkett house was one Sam remembered from her childhood. She'd grown up in this neighborhood, had ridden her bike through its winding streets, past mansions with gazebos and parklike yards. But even for Tuxedo Park, old Clyde Castle was something special—with crenelated towers, turrets, and a moat.

She pulled up to the little guardhouse where an electronic scanner registered the presence of her car.

"Yes, please?"

The disembodied voice was male and decidedly British.

"Samantha Adams to see Mrs. Burkett."

"Could you turn your face more to the left, please?"

She did, then heard a whirring. There was a brief pause.

"Please drive through, Ms. Adams."

The heavy ornamental wrought-iron gates, very pretty and very effective, swung open slowly to allow her to pass, then began to close immediately.

The cobblestone drive led her past formal gardens with low hedges planted in a series of fleurs-de-lis. The house was brick and stone with carved marble ornaments. An equestrian statue sat above the double nail-studded front doors, which opened as she switched off her ignition. A butler in a black coat and striped trousers popped out of the doors.

"Good evening, Ms. Adams. Madame is in her study. If you'll follow me?"

Yes indeed. Right on her tippy toes. The whole setup was like an old movie. Any minute now an ax murderer was going to jump out of a suit of armor.

She ran her lines—how she was going to play the scene with Nicole Burkett, though from their phone conversation she didn't sound like she was going to keel over.

She couldn't wait to hear what the lady did have to say, and what suggestions she might offer. God, she'd be glad to get shut of this mess. What was she thinking about poking around it in the first place? That's what came of having a little free time, no major story cooking. She liked the issues clearer. Murder, for example, had none of this moral ambiguity.

Sam followed the butler across several acres of Aubusson carpeting, past a drawing room, a library; then he stopped and motioned her forward. It was quite a grand view from the gallery to the round room below—Madame's study. She waited for a salute of trumpets—no such luck. Heavy wooden beams curved up to the middle of a pale ivory domed ceiling. Walnut paneling to about shoulder height was carved with a double-folded and pleated linen pattern. Very Francis I. Very elegant. And *very* dear.

"Ms. Adams."

She turned once, twice, looking for the source of Nicole Burkett's voice.

"I'm over here."

Indeed she was, materializing from behind a screen emblazoned with likenesses of Pegasus, the flying horse.

And she was ever more stunning—one of the most beautiful

women Sam had ever seen—blond, blue eyed, somewhere between Catherine Deneuve and Princess Grace, with that same kind of glacial perfection. Then Nicole Burkett pushed a button and her wheelchair scooted forward.

"I was busy at my desk. Always the paperwork. Do you find it so, too?"

Sam nodded and swallowed hard. Nothing in the computer data had prepared her for the wheelchair.

"A riding accident a few years ago." Nicole was reading her mind. "My beloved Windstar misjudged a hurdle, shattered a leg, and had to be shot."

And you didn't.

"And I didn't. Now," she said and pressed another button on the chair's console and spoke into the air, "Drinks, please, Edward."

Sam clocked him at forty-five seconds. In, out, and she was holding a crystal glass filled with Perrier, thank you very much, and a slice of lime. Nicole sipped blond Lillet with a slice of orange, a fine French vermouth and one of Sam's favorites in the bad old days. The Limoges platter Edward had placed between them was decorated with red tuna carpaccio, tiny pasties with oyster mushrooms, checkerboard green and orange vegetable pâté. Food as art.

"How lovely."

"My chef is Japanese, trained in Paris."

"Ah."

"Please. Help yourself. You don't have to feel guilty about enjoying my food even if you've come to break my heart."

Was it a good line because it was delivered by that perfect mouth with that charming accent—or was it just a good line?

"What makes you think I am?"

"An urgent matter concerning a member of my family is not going to be good news. You could have sent a telegram if Miranda had won an award. Or a lottery."

The woman knew she had one foot in the abyss, and still—such charm.

Nicole was wearing buttery Italian leather pumps of magenta.

Resting on the bright chrome step of the wheelchair, they looked brand new. They always would.

Both feet in the abyss.

Then, with a heavy gold lighter, Nicole lit a long, thin brown Turkish cigarette and exhaled through her nose.

"Now, tell me," she said.

Sam studied the ceiling. She focused on a little golden angel at the center where all the beams came together.

This hesitation wasn't like her. She enjoyed a rep for coming right at you—the antithesis of the indirection she'd been taught as a Southern girl. But now, sitting in this beautiful room in her old neighborhood with a woman who reminded her more than a little of her long-dead mother, she found herself going the long way around.

"A week or so ago I got a tip from a friend who works plainclothes with the police department," she began, spinning it out as if she were telling Nicole a story about someone else. The visit to Tight Squeeze. The Japanese tourists. The man offering her money to dance. Seeing Jane Wildwood. Hoke giving Jane a job. Holding back the list with Miranda's name on it. She was all over the map here, but Nicole Burkett let her go, sipping and smoking as if they were old friends enjoying a leisurely visit.

Then Nicole asked, "Have you ever met my daughter?"

"No. But I saw her at a party at the Players."

"The Macbeth party."

"Yes."

"Margaret Landry is stunning in the play, isn't she?"

"Fabulous," Sam agreed.

Were they going to do movie reviews next?

"I've known Margaret for a long time."

There was something else there, right on the tip of Nicole's tongue, but Sam could see her holding back.

Then Nicole focused the beam of her sky-blue gaze. "And what was my daughter doing at the party to make you notice her?"

"She was talking with Laura Landry."

"Ah. And what were they talking about?"

With that, Sam told her. Laid it right out. What Laura had

implied about Miranda and the club. About the list Jane had given her.

Nicole didn't even blink. "Like mother, like daughter," she murmured.

What?

"I beg your pardon?"

"Nothing. I was talking to myself." Nicole shook her head. Not a hair in her silvery-blond chignon stirred. Then she seemed to make up her mind about something. "What did your inquiries tell you about me?"

"Not much. Nothing between your birthdate in Paris and your marriage to Mr. Burkett. Big blank in the middle."

"Did you find that curious?"

"*Very* curious."

"But not enough to pursue it?"

"You aren't the subject of my concern here."

Nicole nodded. "Of course. And what have you decided to pursue? Or not to pursue? I assume you wouldn't have come to me if you were going to spread this story all over the front page of the *Constitution.*"

"No, I wouldn't."

"Did Miss Wildwood give you my name?"

"Yes."

"And what did she tell you?"

"She just said that I should call you."

"Yes." Nicole smiled. "That sounds like something Jane would do."

"She did suggest that you might help me with a solution."

"About what to do if you don't do the story?"

"Yes."

"I will. I'll take care of everything. Consider the matter closed."

Then she extended her hand. The emerald-cut diamond could knock your eyes out. "Thank you for all you've done. And thank you for coming to me. Mr. Burkett and I will be forever grateful to you."

Sam stood, knowing that she was being dismissed. And *handled,* as she'd been throughout the interview, which was fine with her.

As long as Nicole Burkett took care of the dirty linen. But she couldn't quite let go.

"So you *are* going to shut them down?"

"Rest assured."

"Good. And the girls?"

"Ms. Adams, my daughter is one of those girls. Everything will be taken care of. Don't worry. You've done the right thing."

"Okay. Of course. So, good-bye now." Sam turned and then turned again. Nicole hadn't moved an inch, as if she were anticipating the next question. "I don't understand why you didn't know about this. You obviously have resources and know how to use them."

"I try not to meddle in my children's business. Particularly Miranda's."

Sam shrugged. It wasn't much of an explanation.

Nicole could see that. "It's very complicated. The relationship. When this—this *business* is all finished, maybe we'll have another drink and I'll tell you about it."

"Fine. Oh, I almost forgot." Sam reached in her bag. "You'll want this list of owners of the club. Though Jane said they're probably fronts, covering for someone else."

Nicole shook her head. "I won't need it."

Okay. Right. Sure. She knew there was no point in asking why. She was beginning to get the drift that Nicole Burkett's sources and solutions were a hell of a lot more efficient than her computer.

"Good-bye now," her hostess said. "And thank you."

"Thanks for the drink. And—well, you have my number."

She was going to die if she didn't find out how this all ended. Nicole knew that. She nodded. "I'll call you."

Twelve

"George, pass the biscuits, please," asked Sam at the breakfast table the next morning.

"Here you are, my dear. Trade you for an update."

"Well, I had a most interesting visit yesterday with Nicole Burkett, P.C.'s wife. What do you know about her?"

At that, Horace spilled the coffee he was pouring.

"Wait." Sam laid a hand on her uncle's arm. "I've obviously asked the wrong person. Horace, did you want to get in here?"

"Well, I don't know, but there *are* those who say it's peculiar the lady seemed to arrive in this town with no baggage. She's hardly ever seen in public. Ask her a question about the past and she just smiles that pretty smile—is what I hear."

"Arrived full grown as if from the head of Zeus," George added.

"And those who would say she has some interesting friends," Horace continued, "especially for a lady who doesn't get out much."

"Interesting how?"

"Shady."

"Big shady or little shady?"

"Big shady." George beat Horace to it.

"*Excuse* me," Sam said. "The two of you are sitting here, telling me over grits and sausage that P.C. Burkett's wife is hooked up with—shall we say an *underground* source of protection?"

The mob had never been a very visible force in Atlanta, though here, as in every big city, its presence was understood.

"Did you say that?" George asked Horace.

Horace looked around is if there were someone else in the room. "I don't think so."

"But that's what you're implying. Am I right?"

"I'm just telling you what folks say," Horace said. "They could be wrong. Folks don't know everything."

Sam snorted. For the most part, what Horace's *folks* didn't know wasn't worth spit.

"Well, hell," Sam said and reached for another biscuit. "More power to her. At least it's out of my hands."

"That Tight Squeeze matter?" George asked.

"Yep."

"What are you talking about?" asked Horace.

"You got time?"

He nodded and sat down. Sam poured him a cup of coffee, then filled them both in about her meeting with Nicole Burkett.

"I wouldn't want to be in their shoes." Horace shook his head when she was finished. "Those, whoever they are, who're responsible for this mess. Not with Miz Burkett on their tails."

"Hurry up in there," Peaches called from the kitchen through the swinging door. "I've got a meeting to go to and I'm late already."

"I mourn the loss of gentility in the world." George sighed. "You can't even depend on being allowed the pleasures of a little conversation and a good cup of coffee."

With that, Peaches marched into the breakfast room and snatched both their plates away. "You can depend on the fact that people've got better things to do than wait while you lollygag around at the breakfast table, gossiping. Now I happen to know that Nicole Burkett has always been helpful to the unfortunate in this city and I won't have you besmirching her good name."

"No doubt she gave the literacy program a sizable donation," Sam theorized to the blackberry jam.

"She most certainly did, for your information, and if you want anything else, please help yourselves. I'm gone."

"Which means Nicole could be Jack the Ripper and Peaches would defend her all the way to the gallows," said Sam.

"She's done the best she could—nothing lots of other women haven't," Peaches snapped back through the closing door.

"And what's that?" Sam called.

For an answer, Peaches turned the dishwasher on. Then, through the whooshing and churning, they heard the back door slam.

"Shall I make some more coffee?" Horace asked, oblivious to Peaches, which was how they'd managed to stay married for fifty years.

"Thanks, no. Please don't let us keep you from getting on with your day, Horace," said George.

"Just one more thing." Sam stopped him. "No, two."

"Yes?"

"One, is Randolph Percy still staying at the Claridge Club?"

"Last I heard."

"Good. I'm going to see if I can find him this morning right after I make my calls. Two, you remember the other day when we were talking about Felicity Edwards?"

"I do."

"And something came up about maybe she'd had a baby?"

"Yes."

"Well?"

Horace pulled his favorite Braves cap out of his back pocket and settled it on his head. He wore it for chauffering, but felt it helped his cogitation, too.

"It was a really long time ago. And there's never been any proof of it. But there were—"

"—folks who said—" Sam interjected.

"—that that's the reason Miss Emily went up to New York and why Miss Felicity came home with her. That she left a baby up there."

"What do you think?"

"I don't know. I'm just telling you—"

"I know. What folks said."

Sam liked to do all her phone calling in the morning, catching people before they'd had time to get ensnared in their day.

One. Beau had rung her the previous evening, but by the time she got home she hadn't been able to reach him. In a clinch somewhere, no doubt, with some sweet young thing.

"Dr. Talbot, please. Samantha Adams."

"Sammy!"

He'd gotten lucky, all right. He was never this cheerful in the morning.

"So what about the puppy?"

"No 'Good morning, Beau? How are you this beautiful morning?' "

"Good morning, Beau. How are you this beautiful morning? So what about the puppy?"

He made a *tsking* sound. "Can't find a thing. But then, I don't know what the hell I'm looking for. Puppies die, Sammy, usually one in every litter. Natural selection. Mother Nature."

"Screw Mother Nature."

"Boy, did you get up on the wrong side of the bed!"

"I did not. I'm just not willing to let this go because Emily's sure it means something—part of a chain—and now I've got to call her and tell her to blame it on Mother Nature. You want me to quote you on that?"

"Undetermined causes."

"Great. Thanks a lot, Beau."

"Christ. I can't make it up, you know."

"Why don't you run a few more procedures? Keep trying?"

"And I have a few other things to do with my time."

"Oh yeah? I bet. And you never did get back to me on what Beth had to say about Miranda Burkett."

She could hear him smack himself in the forehead with his open hand.

"I swear, I've been running so, I haven't—"

"It's okay, Beau. It's all right. I've taken care of it."

"No, really, I'll call her right—"

"Done. Finished. Don't worry your pretty little head about it."

He growled like a dog.

"Never gonna be part of a team if you can't keep up with the pace, Talbot. Listen, gotta dash. I'll check with you later."

Two. Emily answered on the first ring. Sam told her what Beau had said.

"Oh, dear. Well, I'm sure he thinks I'm a dotty old lady."

"He does no such thing. He's embarrassed because he fell down on the job. He'll stick with it."

"You're going to so much trouble for us, Sam. I don't know how we're ever going to thank you."

"Don't be silly. How's Felicity?"

"No better, I'm afraid. If I could just get her stabilized on her medication again. But she insists on that swill of Mr. Percy's."

"How *is* that gentleman?"

"Well, I'm afraid I wouldn't use such a polite appellation. But to answer your question, I don't know. He hasn't been around for a couple of days."

"Maybe his ardor's cooled. This could be a good sign."

"I wish I could count on it. Wouldn't that be wonderful?" Emily sighed. "But that would probably mean that he'd given up here and was off searching for another goose to produce his golden egg. Some other poor woman who might not have anyone to defend her."

"You're absolutely right. Well, I'm hot on his trail. The newspaper's morgue should have clips for me today, and if there's anything there, I'll add it to my ammunition. I'm going to see him."

"Today?"

"Yep. Hoping to catch him in."

"Are you sure that's a good idea?"

"What do you mean, Emily?"

"I don't know. I guess I'm afraid if he's confronted directly, he might—well, there's no telling what he might do. I'm awfully worried about Felicity."

"I know you are, but I do think I ought to go and see him. We can't just pussyfoot around with this forever. The man needs to be told to bug off."

"I'm sure you're right. And I'm sure you're the one to do it."

But she didn't sound so sure. What the hell was her hesitancy about? Emily was the one who'd told her about Percy in the first place. Well, maybe she was scared. After all, she was an *old* lady.

"I wish you luck."

"You don't think he can be scared off, Emily?"

And as she asked, she had a vision of who might best put the heat on Percy—short, dark guys in overcoats with strategic bulges under their arms—if what Horace said about Nicole's associates were true. Wouldn't hurt to ask. After all, the lady owed her. And what was the point of having connections if they couldn't do you a little favor? She shook her head. She'd been watching too many gangster movies.

"I don't know if he can be scared off or not. Surely other people have gotten on to him. And there's no way of knowing what he's done."

"Well, I'm off to beard him in his den. I'm loaded for bear. Hold down the fort and any other metaphors you can think of. I'll keep you posted."

Three. The morgue did not have her clips yet.

"Miss Cahill said that you were overextended in your requests for the month," said the clerk in that office.

"I didn't know there was a quota on—" She bit her tongue. No point in munching on an innocent by-stander. "Transfer me to Ms. Wildwood, please."

"Hoke Toliver's office. Jane Wildwood speaking."

"You do that very nicely, Wildwood."

"Thanks. You wanna know what else I've learned to do?"

"I'm sure it's fascinating, but some other time. Right now I want you to track down Shirl the Squirrel and cut out her gizzard."

"Roger. And after that?"

"Get me my goddamned clips from the morgue on Randolph Percy."

"That's Percy with a final *e* or without? Going back how far?"

"Without. Forever."

"By the way, Hoke's trying to pump me about what you might be working on. He said you teased him with something. Is he talking Squeeze?"

"Yeah. Now I'm going to have to come up with something else. I put the kibosh on *that* business."

"The whole show?"

"I'm not sure. It's out of my hands."

"See? I told you that you'd like Nicole Burkett."

"Well, I did. She's a very impressive lady, as I'm sure you know. And how *do* you know her, anyway?"

"One of the things I've learned in my on-the-job training is to protect my sources."

"Not from me, Wildwood. I'm your mentor, remember?"

"From everyone."

"Then you'd better learn to protect your ass, too."

"Only teasing, Sam. I'll fill you in later. Now what do you want me to tell Hoke when he asks for you?"

"Tell him—"

"Never mind. I'll make it up. Here comes the Squirrel. Got to get my gun loaded."

The only nice thing a woman could say about the Claridge Club is that it serves a hell of a glass of iced tea. Beyond that, this holy of holies of male supremacy (unscathed by any and all legislation), which sits atop a bank building just across the street from the offices of the *Constitution*, is a thorn under the saddle—a reminder of how everything used to be.

Sam had been inside once before to a Wednesday-Night Dinner to which ladies are admitted. She'd looked up and down the long table—being one of three women in a sea of male faces, all of them white—and thought, *So this is what it feels like.*

Besides which, the food was awful.

Spearing something gray on her fork, she'd said to the man who'd been so foolish as to invite her, "Is this what you all call mystery meat? Or is it shit on a shingle?"

The collective gasp had been heard fifteen miles away in Alpharetta.

She hadn't been invited back to the Claridge. But because Randolph Percy met the criteria for membership, being a gentleman in addition to a con man, a gambler, and a possible murderer, and because he stayed there when he was in Atlanta, she now found herself once again ringing the club's doorbell.

Just inside, she was met by a functionary who had both the shape and demeanor of a boiled egg.

"Yes, ma'am?"

"I wonder if I might see Mr. Randolph Percy?"

"I'll inquire," he said and nodded his perfectly bald head. Nothing else moved. "Please make yourself comfortable in the lounge." Not even his lips. He'd have given Edgar Bergen a run for his money.

Then he ushered her through double doors into the area where ladies in waiting were allowed.

A green overstuffed chair gave off a faint cloud of dust as she plopped into it—probably the biggest event in this room in forty years. It was a place to count flies, leaf through old *National Geographics,* watch fat men sleep, research styles in snoring. The man on her right, who had his head thrown back so far it looked like it might unhinge, was practicing a variation that might appeal to a horny lady hippopotamus.

A side door opened and Mr. Egg returned. "Mr. Percy is not in his room, ma'am."

"Oh, I'm sure he is."

"Ma'am?"

His eyebrows lifted a quarter of an inch—the equivalent for him of a wild Watusi.

"I said I'm sure Mr. Percy is in."

And she was positive. She knew he was upstairs. She could smell him. The sixth sense that she shared with George had just kicked in.

"Did you knock on his door?"

"I rang him." He sniffed.

She was half out of her chair. "Why don't you let me go up and see?"

"Oh, no!" The man jerked back. "I couldn't let you do that. Above stairs is off limits to ladies."

"Then would you please go up and find him? Maybe he's visiting in someone else's room."

Mr. Egg rolled his eyes ever so slightly.

"I am not one of his women, if that's what you think."

"Ma'am?"

"I'm much too young, don't you think?"

No response. Well, sarcasm didn't always work.

"I'm here on business." She dug in her bag and handed him her card. "Please."

He stared at it, and then his eggy face slid like one, over easy. Publicity, of any sort, was anathema to the club.

"I'll be right back." He turned, then paused. A light had gone on. "In the meantime, may I send you something from the bar?"

She smiled sweetly. "A glass of iced tea would be nice."

She remembered the tea from her previous visit. It was brewed fresh and strong and came in a tall glass in a silver holder with lump sugar and lemon on the side and a sprig of real mint.

It hadn't changed. She stirred in the sugar and thought about her strategy.

Mr. Percy, you have forty-eight hours to get the hell out of Dodge.

A little crude but not bad.

"Samantha Adams! What a nice surprise."

She turned and there stood short, fat Judge Deaver. When first they'd met, he'd been perched on the edge of a sofa at a cocktail party, staring down the bosom of a tall redhead built rather like Jane.

"How are you doing, my dear?"

"Fine, and you?"

Behind Deaver stood a tall, distinguished man who looked vaguely familiar.

"Frank O'Connor." He smiled and extended his hand.

"*Judge* O'Connor. Of course."

"Guilty, I'm afraid."

Sam reflexively ran a hand through her curls, then she licked her lips. Well, he was *very* sexy for an old man, tall and broad shouldered with a mane of white hair. No wonder they called him God O'Connor behind his back.

"Whatever are you doing in this stodgy old den? Deaver drags me here once a year, though I keep telling him I disapprove of the place. Could we take you out of here for a breath of fresh air, buy you a proper drink?"

"I'd love to, but I'm here on business."

"Of course. By the way, I want to tell you how much I appreciate the concern you've shown for my friend Emily Edwards and her sister Felicity."

"Oh, well, it's—"

"It's a lovely gesture. And let's hope everything turns out fine with Felicity." He leaned closer. "You wouldn't be here to see that scoundrel Randolph Percy, would you?"

"As a matter of fact—"

"No need to answer. You know, I should have done something about having that sorry bastard, excuse my French, run out of town a long time ago. Well, it's never too late."

Was God O'Connor Emily's *special* friend?

Good for her. From what she'd seen lately, life among the septuagenarians was hotter than she'd ever imagined. Certainly hotter than her own.

Now Mr. Egg was back, standing before them with a most peculiar expression on his face.

"Good day, Rumson," Deaver said.

"Day, sir. *Ahem.*" He cleared his throat and focused a yellow-green gaze on Sam.

"Well?"

"He is in his room, Ms. Adams, but—"

"Just as I thought. He's on his way down?"

"No, I'm afraid not. He's—"

"You gave him my card?"

"No, ma'am. You see—"

She'd run fresh out of patience. "Why the hell not?"

"What seems to be the problem?" O'Connor asked.

"The lady asked if I would ring up a member, sir, and I did, but there was no answer. Then she asked if I would go upstairs and find him. I've done so."

"And? I can't believe a gentleman would be so rude. But then, you didn't give him the card. Does he understand that he's keeping a lady waiting?"

"No, sir, he doesn't."

Rumson's mouth was working sideways in a very strange fashion.

"I don't get it. Why didn't you give him my card?"

"I couldn't, ma'am."

"And may I ask why not? Is Mr. Percy indisposed?" Deaver chimed in.

"Well, yes, he is, sir, ma'am, in a manner of speaking." Then he turned back to Sam. "It was impossible to disturb him. You see, ma'am, I'm terribly afraid Mr. Percy's dead."

Thirteen

Sam waited in the foyer until the police arrived, two uniformed officers followed closely by another couple of homicide detectives. They argued among themselves for a few minutes over which team would take the call.

"Why don't you flip a coin?" she suggested.

She'd recognized one of the uniforms from her recent visit to Charlie at headquarters. Now he picked her out, too.

"That's not exactly SOP, Ms. Adams. You grab the squeal on the radio?"

"No, actually I was here to see Mr. Percy about a little business."

He glanced down at the notebook he was holding.

"This same Percy?"

She nodded.

"Isn't that a neat coincidence? Hope it wasn't important."

"Not anymore it isn't."

"You coming up with us?"

"Why, thank you."

What a nice surprise, to be invited to a crime scene. Usually she had to coax, cajole, and muscle her way in.

All five of them, six including Rumson, began to troop up the stairs.

"Your friend Charlie said we should be nice to you; you'd write sweet things about us. Help with our image."

"Why, I always do. I'm one of the department's biggest fans." Actually that was true.

But it didn't play well to this audience, conditioned to mistrust the press. One of the other cops made a rude sound as they all followed Rumson up the stairs.

At the top, Rumson turned to the right. "This way." He pointed. They followed single file along a worn Persian runner, then stood crowded at the doorway of room fourteen while Rumson unlocked it.

The room was much too small to accommodate all of them—not that they all rushed in at once to meet the sickly sweet smell that greeted them. Sam reached in her bag for a tissue to press over her nose as she peeked in at the simple furnishings: a single bed with an oak headboard, a matching dresser, a night table with a brass lamp, a chair upholstered in green tweed. It looked like a dorm room. And Randolph Percy looked like he'd stretched out for the night.

His last outfit was a pair of pale blue pajamas, monogrammed in navy on the breast pocket. His hands lay at his sides over the bedspread, the nails neatly manicured and lightly polished, a gold crested ring on one finger. His silver hair winged back from a high forehead. His nose was aquiline, his features strong and fine. Even dead, he was a good-looking man. Sam was sorry she hadn't had a chance to meet him.

"He didn't answer when I knocked," Rumson said. "But the door was unlocked."

"Is that unusual?" one of the homicide dicks asked.

"No, sir. This is a gentlemen's club. There's no need to be concerned about security."

The detective's face registered his skepticism. "So you opened the door and walked in?"

"Yes, sir. And then I saw Mr. Percy sleeping. At least, I thought he was sleeping."

"And?"

"Well, it seemed a little irregular. I mean, Mr. Percy was never one to lie about in the daytime, if you know what I mean, sir. Unless he was ill, perhaps."

"So you tried to wake him."

"I did, sir. I called his name several times, each time more loudly."

"And when he didn't stir?"

"That's when I touched him." Rumson shuddered involuntarily.

"And you realized he was cold."

"Yes, sir. Quite cold. Of course, I noticed the—" He was embarrassed to mention it.

"The smell? I'd say he's been here a while. Did you touch anything else?"

"Nothing except the door. I locked it, seemed the right thing to do, and went straight downstairs and told Ms. Adams, who'd come to see him—and Judges Deaver and O'Connor who were talking with her. And then we called you."

"What did you say your business was with Percy?" the heftier of the two detectives asked Sam.

"I didn't." She smiled. "But I will—"

However, not just then, for at that moment, Beau Talbot and Lee Boggs, one of his investigators, made their way into the official crush.

"Samantha." Beau nodded.

"Dr. Talbot. Mr. Boggs." She nodded back.

"Good to see you, Sam," said Boggs, a sweet-faced man of whom Sam was quite fond. A terrier at a crime scene, he looked like a Sunday school teacher.

"I believe the rest of us know each other," Beau continued, then turned his attention inside the room. "I was having lunch, didn't get any particulars with the call from the Fulton County M.E. This must be a hot one if they're passing it to us."

"Probably the club," Sam offered.

When a case might be political, and at the Claridge everything was potentially political, strings would be pulled and the Georgia Bureau of Investigation, of which Beau's office was a part, would be given the high sign.

He jerked a thumb at the corpse. "Do we know the identity of the gentleman?"

"Name's Randolph Percy," said one of the cops.

"Percy?" Beau whistled, then turned and gave Sam a look. "A little drastic, don't you think, Sammy?"

"What?" The beefy detective looked from one to the other. "What do you mean?"

"Sam'll explain it all to you later," said Beau. "Won't you?"

She narrowed her eyes at Beau in warning. He was so obnoxious when he got to play super doc. But he also could be awfully useful.

"So what do you think?" she asked him.

"You mean from just standing here six feet away? You're asking for my professional opinion?"

"I thought you'd gotten so good at this you could just sniff the scene. Like a bird dog."

There was a little sound behind her. The cops were enjoying this.

"What do you think, Boggs?" Beau asked.

The senior technician who'd stepped past everyone else had been gently probing the body, carefully inspecting the bed, the floor, touring the private bathroom, doing a routine preliminary scan of a potential crime scene.

"Nothing," he answered.

"Nothing," Beau said. "No sign of a struggle, nothing out of order. No forced entry. I'd say the old man died in his sleep. From the aroma, a couple of days ago."

"Well, you'll find out in the autopsy," Sam said. Four beats. "Probably."

"We might. And we'll be sure and give you a call. We want you to be among the first to know the cause of death."

"Why, thank you." She smiled.

One of the cops sniggered.

"I'll be through here in a few minutes," said Boggs, who'd been busy with his camera.

"Good," said Beau. "Then we'll take the body in."

"This is perfectly dreadful," Rumson murmured beside Sam.

"Did you know Randolph Percy well?" She was hauling out her notebook, pen poised, ready to record his story.

"No. Not really." He looked surprised. "Oh, I didn't mean that. I meant perfectly dreadful for the club. Couldn't we keep this out of the paper?"

Fourteen

"Well, I wish I could say I was sorry." Emily Edwards pushed her tortoise-shell glasses to the top of her head and pulled her knees up to her chest. She and Sam were sitting on the Edwardses' back steps. "That's a terrible admission, isn't it? To be glad someone's dead?"

"Not in this case. Bastard just saved me from calling in a favor."

Though, in truth, she'd rather fancied the idea of asking Nicole Burkett to inveigle her friends to lean on Percy.

"Poor Felicity," Emily continued. "Even though it's for the best, she's not going to take this well. She thought Randolph hung the moon." Emily stood, then covered the short distance to the front of one of the dog runs. "Hush, girl," she ordered a spaniel who was barking at a salamander. "Well, maybe I can get Felicity to the doctor and back on her medication now. All that junk of Randolph's ever did was make her a little tiddly, and well, you've seen what happens when she's off her lithium."

"What do you think was in Randolph's elixir?"

"I *know* what it was. Alcohol. Food coloring. A few herbs. I tried some myself. Perfect nonsense—like other patent medicines. Hadacol. Do you remember that?"

"I do. A housekeeper we had once gave it to me. It tasted terrible, but I loved it."

"Of course you did. It made you drunk."

"See? They put it in my bottle. Started me early on the road to perdition."

"I didn't mean—"

"Nonsense. It was my bad joke. But listen, do you still have any of Percy's stuff around?"

"Why, yes. I'm sure there's still a bottle in Felicity's room."

"I think we ought to have Beau take a look at it."

"Of course. But why?"

"Funny feeling—I'm not sure Percy's death was kosher. I think we ought to collect whatever we can on him."

"But you said he died from natural causes."

"I said that's what Beau surmised from looking at his corpse from across the room. We haven't heard the autopsy report yet."

"And you think this elixir had something to do with it? If that were true—" She put her hand to her heart. "Then what about Felicity?"

"Well, she has been stranger and stranger, hasn't she?"

"Yes, but, my dear, you're implying that the draught killed him."

"Now that's an interesting possibility, isn't it?"

"Samantha! Why do you think anyone would kill Randolph Percy?"

"Why, Emily. Lots of people had perfectly good reasons. As you well know, he was a charming but despicable man who preyed on women like Felicity. In fact, you *yourself* had ample reason to kill him."

At that, her gaze and Emily's locked. Emily *did*, didn't she? Especially if Felicity had changed her will to include Randolph, which would mean that Emily's share would be smaller. Or nonexistent. Had Felicity done that? And did Emily know it?

Finally, Emily looked away and laughed. But a bright red spot of color burned on each cheek.

"I guess you'll want to know where I was for the past forty-eight hours."

"Why forty-eight? Is that a magic number?"

"Well, I don't know—I just—now look here, Samantha." Now Emily was really agitated.

"I'm only teasing you."

But she wasn't. Not really. She wasn't going to be able to let go of the idea now that it was planted. Especially since something else had been sowed earlier today. When she'd told Emily she was going to visit Percy, Emily had been so hesitant—as if she didn't want her to go. Was she afraid Percy might not be dead yet? Did her plan really require forty-eight hours?

Though why would Emily call Sam and George in if she were planning to kill Randolph? Why would she want someone poking about in her business? Was she that clever, had she planned it out that far ahead, that no one would possibly suspect her if she'd invited the interference? This train of thought seemed highly unlikely.

Of course, there were lots of people with motives. God only knew how many. Patsy Finch, for one, whom she knew by name, the woman in Decatur who thought he'd killed her mother, who'd been done out of part of her inheritance. The woman's whiny voice echoed in her ears.

Hell, Patsy Finch probably didn't have the energy to kill Percy, even if it meant only slipping him a couple of pills.

There were so many people with motives. She'd have to talk with Dan Clayton in Savannah and see who had filed complaints.

She could just hear him now. "You're crazy, Sam. The bastard's gone—and good riddance. Why do you care who did it?"

A good question.

She was crazy anyway to think there was anything suspicious about Percy's death.

Probably Beau's first guess was right.

Probably he died of natural causes.

If so, then she'd have a clean plate again, wouldn't she?

The Tight Squeeze matter dumped in the lap of Nicole Burkett.

Randolph Percy conveniently dead.

Felicity back on her medication would improve, especially in her sister's capable hands.

But what about the doll and the chocolate, the puppy and the Mother's Day card?

Chalk it all off to Percy. She'd never known exactly what he was up to—but definitely no good.

And Felicity's baby? The one she kept nattering about—that Horace seemed to think had really existed?

So what? It was water under the bridge many years ago. And *none* of her business.

Well, what about Laura Landry?

A pretty young girl who was a friend of Miranda Burkett's and a student of Felicity's. Whom she'd seen talking with Beau at her mother's party. Who'd dropped by for voice coaching. She'd seemed a key—tied to both Miranda and Felicity. But a key to what? There was nothing to solve. Nothing to open. Laura was just what she seemed, a pretty girl who got around town a lot, with many friends and interests. No law against that. Coincidence.

"Samantha?"

"I'm sorry, Emily. Woolgathering."

"I wondered, could I ask you to help me break the news of Randolph's death to Felicity?"

"You killed him," Felicity shrieked at her sister. Blue veins throbbed in her milk-white throat and at her temples. Her face twisted into a witch's mask. "You never wanted me to be happy. You always took away everything and killed it!"

Felicity had been going on this way for ten minutes. No matter what Emily or Sam said or did, she raved. Her hands twisted like snakes. Spittle filled the corners of her mouth. But she didn't leave her chair; she seemed tied to it. Back and forth she rocked, faster and faster. Any minute she might take flight.

"I'd best sedate her," Emily whispered. "Will you stay here with her a few minutes?"

"Of course." Sam nodded. *Sedate* her? But of course, Emily was a nurse. She'd done it before. She did it all the time.

Felicity rocked faster and faster.

"She was a little girl," she said. "A beautiful little girl. I saw her. She says I didn't, but I remember. I counted all her fingers and toes. She was perfect. Then Emily took her away and killed her."

Whoa. What was this? How crazy was she?

Felicity focused her big brimming eyes on Sam, then zeroed in on her. Her voice dropped in pitch.

"I know you don't believe me, Samantha. Nobody does. But I'm not crazy. Believe me, Emily killed my child a long time ago. *Please* believe me."

This was the voice in which Sam had first heard Felicity speak, the voice with the gorgeous modulation, the tumbling brook of a voice that made heads turn, seeking its source.

"I know you don't. Nobody believes me. But I'm not crazy, not all the time."

Now in her mind's eye, Sam saw Emily standing in the little pantry downstairs, reaching into the small refrigerator and pulling out a vial, then slowly and carefully filling a syringe with a cold, clear, lethal liquid. Sam shivered.

She *did* believe Felicity.

Just then, from below, Emily screamed.

"My God! Oh, my God!"

Sam flew, taking the stairs two at a time.

"Dear God!" Emily shrieked again. "What? Why is this happening?"

She stood in the pantry where, moments before, Sam had imagined her. But she held neither a vial nor a syringe. Both her hands were open and empty. She turned and lifted them in a gesture of supplication.

"Look!" she cried, and then both hands flew out, all ten fingers splayed, pointing at the disaster around her.

The long shelves of the pantry had been filled with hundreds of jars of fruits and vegetables, glowing like rubies, emeralds, and yellow topaz. Now they were empty.

The long hours that the Edwards sisters had labored in their hot kitchen with their cook Louise had been a waste, for the jars lay smashed. Emily stood in a sticky stew of goo and broken glass. Not a single jar was left intact.

Nor, finally, was Emily's fortitude.

"Why?" She turned to Sam with tears pouring down her face. "Why here? Why me?"

Fifteen

Later after supper, Sam and George strolled arm in arm through their neighborhood.

"Unless we believe in ghosts, Randolph Percy did not smash all the jars in Emily's and Felicity's pantry," Sam said.

"That's for sure."

"Maybe we can't attribute those other things to him either—the candy, the doll, the Mother's Day card."

"Possibility."

"Or maybe he did *some* of them."

"Yes."

"And somebody else the other."

"Who are we talking about?"

"I don't know." She led George around a clump of yellow chrysanthemums. "Maybe Emily and Percy."

"In cahoots?"

"Emily could have led Percy on, then killed him."

"Why?"

"Maybe Felicity was leaving all her money to charity, to a favorite cause, to the Players, I don't know."

"Maybe Emily loved Percy," George suggested.

"Now there's an idea. Maybe it had nothing to do with money."

"Possible, but I'm having a hard time with it. Emily's one of my favorite people, you know. And didn't you say you thought she was seeing God O'Connor?"

"That's how it seemed from what he said—was that only this morning? Seems years ago."

"Finding dead people does make the day seem longer."

"Humph," she said. "But you know"—she reached out to keep

George from walking into a low-hanging branch—"there's still the fact that I believe Felicity about that damned baby."

"You mean that it existed? You don't suspect Emily of killing an infant, too, do you? Forty, fifty years ago?"

"I don't know. When Felicity said it I believed it."

"She does have that voice."

"You're right. It could convince you of anything."

They walked on. She stared up at the wide, bowed front windows of a white brick mansion, and just at that moment someone inside switched on a light. A couple sat in matching red leather armchairs across from one another. A blond woman held a small child on her knee. All three of them were laughing.

"Maybe Emily smashed all those jars," she said.

"Why?"

"To divert attention from herself."

"*Hmmm.* Or to destroy something."

"Something hidden in one of the jars."

"Yes."

"But if she knew it was there, why not just remove it?"

"Beats me."

"Me, too. I think I'll ask her."

"Not a bad idea."

Streetlights switched on then, casting a yellow glow on the oak-bowered street.

"I miss Mom and Dad most at this time of day," she said.

George didn't bat an eye at her mental hopscotch.

"Especially Mom."

"I know. Me, too." Sam's mother had been his most beloved baby sister.

"Nicole Burkett reminds me of her a little."

"Same hair."

"Same manner. I remember Mommy always being so calm. So in control."

"She was that. But she was a lot of fun too. An awfully jolly girl."

"Didn't she have a great laugh, though?"

They were well past the big white house with the happy family now and were passing a vacant, overgrown lot.

"What was here?" Sam pointed.

George peered into the darkness, remembering more than seeing. "The old Webster house. Burned to the ground. A real tragedy."

"Is there a story? Do I know it?"

"I don't think so. It was a long time ago."

Sam urged him on.

"Jack Webster came home and found his wife in bed with a servant. A man who had lived in for years. So Jack locked them in the bedroom and burned the house down."

"Jesus!"

"Then he drove up to their place on Lake Lanier and blew his brains out. Took all their dogs along. Killed them, too."

"My God!"

"They razed the ruins. But the property has remained in the family. You probably know their son, Houston."

"Sure."

"He couldn't bear to build here or to sell the land, so it's stood. It's all overgrown, isn't it?"

"Like a little forest. As if nothing ever stood there." Two beats. "Boy, Atlanta does have its share of tragedy."

"Every place does."

"Maybe it just seems more dramatic in the South."

"Blood on the moon? Mayhem among the magnolias?"

"Something like that."

"Perhaps you're right."

"I think it's partly because everybody goes around being so polite all the time. Pretending everything's just hunky-dory."

"You mean the crazy-child-locked-up-in-the-attic syndrome? The poor Petersons? Pretending little Peter wasn't there all those years?"

"You laugh. But you know it's true. You've had your share of your Petersons."

"But you must remember, I haven't your perspective, dear. I haven't been away like you. Off."

"Look at Felicity. Properly married to a banker for forty years, crazed by a terrible secret about a baby she had up in New York."

"Well, you don't know that for sure."

She gave him a look.

"It's not like young women haven't been having illegitimate babies since time immemorial, for Christ's sakes. But here it gets all blown out of proportion. Drives you nuts. Drove Felicity nuts," she muttered.

"Her manic-depression had something to do with that."

"Okay. Then let's look at Nicole Burkett."

"Fine. What about her?"

"Well, *what* about her? Woman doesn't have any history from the time she was born until she married P.C. You want to tell me there's not some super-deep dark skulking around there?"

"She's not Southern. Doesn't fit the pattern."

"Christ. Okay. She's married to one of the biggest, richest, most aristocratic good old boys who ever chugged bourbon, but you're right. She's not. But she's sure expected to *be* a Southern lady, isn't she? And there's something back there that she's hiding like crazy, that's not up to snuff. Something that probably contributed to her dear darling daughter's wanting to show off her sweet young body at Tight Squeeze."

"You don't think you're pushing it a little?"

"I do not."

"You think Southern women *in particular* live lives of quiet desperation? Is that what you're saying?"

"Something like that."

She was warning to her subject now, walking ahead of George and turning back around to make her point.

"Let me put it to you this way. Have you ever listened to Southern women talk?"

"My dear, I've spent my whole life here, and I may be going blind, but I'm not deaf. My head is filled with the sound of their voices."

"But do you ever really listen to them? Those high little-girl voices, so full of sweetness and light? Ending every sentence like a question because they don't even feel they have the right to make a declarative statement. Wouldn't say shit if they had a mouth full of it. Oh, sometimes they do, when they're alone, I mean with each other, just a couple of close friends or sisters, then you hear them get down and dirty. But the rest of the time in society, honey, they *know* their husbands are running around on them, they *know* their children are doing drugs, they just keep on pouring tea and baking cookies and smiling. Dressing in fresh, lacy underwear and smiling. Pretending their husbands aren't passed-out drunk on the sofa and smiling."

"You'd rather they did something drastic, took lovers like poor Melba Webster?" He gestured back behind them to the ruin they'd passed. "End up burned to a crisp in bed?"

"Jesus Christ, I don't think that's the only possible ending to that scenario."

"Or more like Mavis Tallbutton, loading up double-barreled shotguns and hijacking buses? Taking the law into their own hands?"

"She didn't shoot anybody."

"I can't believe you said that."

"Well, she didn't. And I bet she felt a hell of a lot better than if she'd sat home rocking on her front porch, pretending that she wasn't pissed as hell at her husband because he wouldn't do a damned thing. And at her sister-in-law and her daughter."

"The daughter who did exactly what she wanted to do."

"Right."

"I think you've argued yourself into a corner."

"I have not! Maureen did what she wanted to and Mavis did the same. And the devil take the hindmost."

"That's not how the world runs. And those Tallbuttons aren't exactly society."

"Then fuck society."

"Whoa! You sound like your friend Julia Townley."

"Yes, I do. And I sound like me."

"Yes, you're right. You do indeed." George chuckled. He did enjoy these conversations in which one or the other of them played the devil's advocate. "You sound a little like your mother, too."

"George, my mother was the consummate Atlanta lady. And she certainly never said *fuck* in her entire life."

"Not in front of her darling little girl, maybe. But she could curse like a sailor when provoked. Your father used to say he found it sexy."

As she had, too—when Sean flew off the handle. Wasn't that funny? Was the quirk congenital?

"We argued ourselves around the block," she said, looking up now at their old familiar house that she so loved.

"So we have indeed. Let's go sit on the side gallery and have a sip."

"And I'll call Beau and see if he knows anything more on the late Mr. Percy."

"Nothing untoward in the autopsy," Beau said.

"So what was it?"

"Old age."

"He wasn't *that* old."

"What's the age at which people are allowed to die of natural causes, Dr. Adams? Seventy? Seventy-five? Eighty? I guess you just feel it in your bones that something's fishy."

"You got it."

"I keep telling you we need to X-ray those pretty bones or send them back to med school."

"Very funny."

"You'll be pleased to know I have someone checking to see if he complained of any symptoms in the last few days. But so far, we've found nothing in the lab. And, yes, we're cross-checking with the puppy's results."

She laughed.

"Wasn't that your next question?"

"Sure."

"See, I keep telling you we'd make a great team, Sammy. You've even got me thinking crooked like you do."

"And it's improved your work, right?"

"I wouldn't go that far. But, anyway, we got zilch. And I still don't know what killed that puppy."

"Really zilch?"

"So far. There are endless procedures, and there's no clue as to where to start. One doesn't perform a good autopsy in a vacuum, you know. And so far, we haven't been able to track down Percy's medical history. This could be something as simple as insulin coma leading to death, but in a person dead for several hours, insulin levels aren't reliable. And we'd place him at at least forty-eight hours. So I wouldn't know about the diabetes, if it were that, for example, without his history."

"Shoot! That reminds me. I meant to bring you some of his crazy tonic."

"I'll be happy to take a look but—"

"*But!* Aren't you going to pursue this?"

"I can't. My most informed opinion really is natural causes. I can't spend the time and money, Sammy, without something more to go on."

"So it's over?"

"It's never over until it's over. I'll save tissue, urine, bile and blood samples. Just because I release the body from the autopsy room to the family doesn't mean that's all the work that can ever be done."

"His family's anxious?"

"His mother's practically sitting outside my door. Wants to take her Randy home. She and the sister."

"The sister! The one from California? She and the mother don't speak."

"Well, they do now. They've set up a tent out there in my lobby, I only let them because they're friends of yours, both of them wailing and carrying on, and I'll tell you, I'm right anxious to get shut of the remains of Mr. Percy."

She ignored the jibe. "Now I wonder why she told me that? That they don't speak?"

"Might not have before now. You just haven't spent enough time around the bereaved, my dear. Hook yourself up with a good funeral parlor around town for a couple of weeks."

"Thanks for the tip, but I'll pass."

"Well, you'll be missing out on some mighty fine stuff. You ain't seen nothing, sugar, until you've seen a real strong grieving family chewing on the bones of the deceased."

"Lovely image, Beau."

"We do our best."

"You know, I'm going to talk with Emily first thing in the morning."

"Beg your pardon?"

"I said Emily Edwards got me into this and, by God, she can get me out of it."

Sam had just settled into bed with Harpo and the latest Elmore Leonard novel when her telephone rang.

"Hi. It's Jane."

"I'm trying to get some rest here."

"It's only nine o'clock. Old before your time, Adams."

"It's been a long day. Full of corpses and busted jam jars."

"Sounds rough. How many jam jars?"

"Okay. So I exaggerated. Only one old charmer named Randolph Percy."

"Haven't had the pleasure—that I know of."

Remembering that she never wanted to read Jane's résumé, Sam let the comment pass.

"So you called me up in the middle of the night to insult me about my age?"

"Actually I called to apologize."

"Great. I love apologies. What for?"

"For not answering your question about Nicole Burkett yesterday."

Sam sat up. "I'm all ears."

Then the phone gurgled and clanked.

"This is a terrible connection. Are you in a phone booth?"

"Uh-huh."

"What's the number?" Then she said, "That's the pay phone at Manuel's," when Jane told her.

"How do you know that?"

"Age," Sam said. "Experience. Stay put. The old lady'll creak right over and buy you a beer."

Five minutes later, Sam walked in the back door of the tavern with a sweat shirt pulled over her T-shirt and a pair of old jeans. Harpo's head poked out of a big bag she was carrying.

"He needed a drink?" Jane asked from the booth she'd snagged in the front room.

"A little excitement. He likes this crowd. Actually he likes any crowd. As the world's cutest dog, he can always depend on lots of admirers."

"Hi, Harpo," said Charles, Sam's favorite waiter, as he delivered her Perrier, unordered, to the table.

See? She grinned at Jane, who ignored her. Then she ordered them each a chili dog and Harpo a burger naked, for starters. "So what's the story?"

"This is off the record."

"Thank you very much, Ms. Wildwood. Remind me to teach you lesson number one. *Nothing* is ever off the record if you need it. You just find another way to use it."

Jane lit a long, brown Turkish cigarette, shades of Nicole Burkett, and exhaled deeply. Was Nicole her mentor, too? If so, in what?

"That's an affectation," Sam said. "That's going to kill you."

"It's not an affectation. I happen to like the taste of these cigarettes."

"Which are going to kill you."

"When are you going to stop mothering me?"

"When you grow up."

Jane flopped her curtain of red hair down and glared at Sam through it.

"Sorry. Forget I said it. Now why'd you get me out of my warm, comfy bed?"

"You ever hear of Constance Bonnet?"

"The Parisian madame?"

"Very good."

"Retired not too many years ago. Recruited the most beautiful young girls in the world, well, the ones who were available, and trained them."

"Right."

"Sent them out by private jet when pashas, Greek shipping

tycoons, arms dealers, royalty of whatever cut got the urge for something young, beautiful, and very special. Never had a house. The girls freelanced."

"Absolutely. You passed the quiz."

"Okay. So give me my reward. What does this have to do with Nicole?"

Jane met her look.

"No."

"Yes."

"Nicole Burkett?"

"She started out as Nicole Chenonceaux. Of *very* humble origins."

"Don't tell me. Her mother was a chambermaid. Her father a duke. A descendant of Louis XIV."

Jane laughed. "I don't know. I just know she grew up about as poor as I did and she was one of Connie's girls."

"And that's how she met P.C.?"

"You got it."

"And he married her?"

"He wouldn't be the first man who ever married a whore."

"Well, shut my mouth. But P.C. Burkett, Mr. Gotrocks from Waycross, Georgia? I'm having trouble getting my mind around it. And how do you know this?"

Jane gave her a look again.

"You're absolutely right. I really don't want to know. I want you to protect that source until the day you die."

Jane grinned. "I intend to."

"So that's Nicole's secret." She waved at Charles. "Dozen oysters, please." Then she rubbed her hands together. "News like this makes me hungry. Listen, it doesn't make any difference, but maybe you know this, too. Does Nicole have connections with the mob? I'm just curious."

Jane shrugged. "Let's just put it this way. P.C. Burkett's not the only man in the world who might want to do her a favor. He's certainly not the first rich and powerful man she ever slept with."

"Nor the last?"

"I didn't say that. I have no idea. Though now . . ." Jane gestured, implying Nicole's injury.

"You think Miranda knows about her mother?"

"Not if Nicole could help it. No. I don't think that's why Miranda got herself involved at Tight Squeeze, if that's what you mean."

"Then why?"

"Why did I?"

"I don't know, Jane."

"I needed the cash. I didn't like myself very much."

"You think Miranda needs money?"

"I don't know. Not unless she has a drug habit."

"Does she?"

"Not that I noticed."

"What about liking herself?"

"Now that is a whole other can of worms. I'm not prepared to speak about her emotional health and well being."

"How about yours?"

"Do I like myself more these days?"

"Yeah."

"You bet. Actually I had become rather enamored of myself some time ago. I was just waiting for Joan of Arc to come along and save me."

"Go fuck yourself, Wildwood." Sam toasted her with a raised glass.

Jane grinned and lifted her beer. "Same to you."

George awoke when she came in later. Much later.

"Sam?" he called from his room.

"It's me. Go back to sleep. I didn't mean to wake you."

"You've been saying that since you were twelve years old. Where'd you go?"

"To meet Jane. Go back to sleep."

"What'd she want?"

"To tell me something about Nicole Burkett."

"What?"

"Probably nothing you didn't already know."

"And nothing you need to go spreading about either," said

Peaches, who just then glided into the hall through the kitchen door. She was carrying a tray with two cups of warm milk, starting back up the stairs to Horace.

"Peaches," Sam said, "can you tell me why it is *I'm* the reporter in this family and *I'm* always the last one to know anything that's of any importance? Wouldn't you think my very own family would fill me in on something just once in a great while?"

Peaches slowed down for an instant and squinted at her. "You would think so."

Sixteen

Peaches didn't really know about Nicole Burkett, Sam said to herself as she drove across town to the offices of Lighthouse for the Blind the next morning. It was Saturday, but that's where Felicity had told Sam she could find Emily. Which was fine, since it would be good to talk with her away from home.
If Peaches did know, wouldn't she tell her?
Maybe not. Peaches was a mean old woman.
No, that wasn't true. She was just crotchety. Set in her ways. And, Sam had to face it, her surrogate mother, which meant their relationship was as wacky as if Peaches had borne her instead of only taken her to raise.
Now what was she holding out about Felicity?

"Samantha! What a nice surprise. Come on into my office." Emily walked from behind her desk, smoothing her khaki skirt, extending her hand. The gracious Southern lady on the job.
"Sorry to drop in on you like this."
"Don't be silly. Can I give you the tour? Get you a cup of coffee?"
"I'll take the coffee, thanks."
"Here, then." Emily pointed at a small table piled with books, flanked by two comfortable chairs. "Why don't you settle yourself, and I'll go scare up the coffee. Just move those things over to the bookshelf. I must do something about this office."
Sam waved her and her apology away and picked up the books.
A volume on seeing-eye dogs.
Another on spaniels.
A report from a conference in Lucerne on the disabled.

The Awakening by Kate Chopin. A wonderful novel about a woman too advanced for her own good. Emily *would* like it. At the bottom of the pile was *The Great Gatsby.*

Sam sat down with the book and leafed through the pages of one of her old favorites.

The elusive Jay Gatsby and his long-lost Daisy with her melodious Southern voice. As Fitzgerald said, a voice full of money.

That was who Felicity had always reminded her of, Fitzgerald's Daisy Buchanan. Daisy of the astonishing voice. Lovely, careless, selfish Daisy who ran down her husband's lover in Gatsby's roadster, then let Gatsby take the blame.

Sam started.

Why not?

For suddenly it occurred to her that she might be barking up the wrong Edwards sister.

What if Felicity's madness were a charade?

What if Felicity had planted the incidents that pointed away from her?

What if Felicity killed Randolph Percy?

But why?

Because he was the long-ago deserting father of her child?

Because he was blackmailing her?

Over what?

That secret, the baby. Or some other.

Or perhaps there was something between Emily and Randolph. Felicity's jealousy was the motive. Maybe that was it.

Just then Emily bustled back into the room with two steaming mugs. "You do take it light, don't you, dear?"

"Thank you."

"Now, to what do I owe this pleasure? Something about Mr. Percy?"

Sam sipped the coffee.

Then her eyes met Emily's.

"I'm afraid I'm here to ask you some hard questions."

"Well, yes." Emily sighed. "I knew you would eventually." She planted the mug firmly on the table and crossed her hands in her lap, assuming the demeanor of someone finally roped into the dentist's chair. "Go ahead. Do your duty."

This was going to be easier than Sam had thought.

Maybe.

"I can't shake the feeling that the imaginary baby Felicity talks about is important here."

"To Percy?"

"To Percy. To Felicity. It figures somewhere."

Emily sighed.

"Does it, Emily?"

"I'm afraid it might. Sort of indirectly."

"So there was a baby."

"Yes." She fiddled with the handle of her mug. "There was. I knew you'd realize that sooner or later. Yes. Felicity *did* have a baby." Then she leaned back and Sam watched as her body relaxed. There. Fifty-odd years. She'd finally said the words.

"When?"

"In 1937, in New York. She was twenty-two. It was a disaster. She could have gone far." Emily shook her head. "I hate waste."

"Why did that stop her? I know it was a different time, but I wouldn't think a child would necessarily end her career."

"Because that was when her manic-depressive cycles began in earnest."

"You mean the shock of the baby's death brought them on?"

Emily's head snapped.

Uh-oh. She'd gone too far too fast. Nobody had said anything about the baby dying. At least nobody here today. That had been Felicity who'd said Emily had killed the child. Not exactly what one wanted to bring up at this juncture.

"Noooo." Emily drew the word out, all the while playing with the heavy gold chain she wore around her neck and the engraved locket-watch suspended from it. "No," she repeated, "the pregnancy triggered the cycles. The change in hormones. You know, women experience all kinds of aberrations in their bodies during and after pregnancy. Curly hair goes straight. Allergies they never had before. Multiple sclerosis. Pregnancy can be very dangerous. And in Felicity's case, it was." Then she smiled slightly as if she knew she wasn't going to get away so easily. "So it wasn't the fact that she thought the baby died that brought on the manic-depression. Though that certainly didn't help."

"What do you mean *thought?*"

Emily's eyes suddenly went big. Here it came.

"The baby didn't die. I mean, I told her that the baby didn't make it. But she did."

"A girl."

"A beautiful little girl."

"What happened to her?"

"Nothing catastrophic. Her grandparents raised her."

"But wouldn't—"

"No, no." Emily shook her head. "On her father's side. The baby grew up with that family."

"And Felicity's daughter's alive now?"

Sam had done the calculation earlier. She'd be in her early fifties.

"No. I don't know." Emily fidgeted with the locket, snapped it open and shut. "It was better that Felicity thought she was dead, so she wouldn't have to worry about her the rest of her life. And I didn't want to know either. Her grandparents were good people. I helped them with her financially. Other than that, I don't know anything. I don't know what happened to her." Her voice was so low at the end that Sam could barely hear her.

"Emily," she said, "as respectfully as I know how, I have to tell you that I think you're lying. Or at least sidestepping."

Emily turned her head, staring at the walls as if she'd never seen them before, at diplomas and awards inscribed with her name. At photographs of herself, young and old, in whites, in khaki, and in street clothes, smiling in a variety of groupings. Emily in her early fifties standing next to a grinning John Fitzgerald Kennedy.

"It's the same thing, isn't it? And I'm not very good at it."

"Nope."

"I've never been good at deception." Then she turned back and looked Sam straight in the eye. "Except those years in the camp in the Philippines." She pointed a forefinger. "I was *very* good then."

"I bet you were."

"Please don't patronize me."

"I'm not. Nothing could be further from my intent, Emily. I think you're a courageous woman. And whatever this is that you've hidden for so long, I know it's been very hard for you."

"It has. But there's no excuse for it, for my behavior, for the lies." She stood now, straightening her backbone, and strolled back and forth in a short path between her desk and the table. "They were wrong, and they made it harder for everyone. Especially for Margaret."

"I beg your pardon?"

"Margaret Landry." Emily's eyes drilled into Sam's then, her head high, her jaw strong. "My niece. Felicity's daughter."

"His name was Johnny Jackson. Hoppin' John was his nickname —the name he used on stage."

Emily was telling it all now. She couldn't be stopped once she'd started. Sam had already gotten up once and found the place down the hall, poured them each another cup of coffee. She didn't want Emily to move. Just keep talking.

"He was an actor?"

"A musician. Jazz musician. He played the saxophone, I believe. No, the clarinet. That's right." And then her eyes went away somewhere. "We used to go and listen to them in a club on West Fifty-second Street. Late at night, till the wee hours. A small room filled with smoke, women in satin dresses, *that* music." She smiled.

"It was really something, huh?"

"Yes, it was. Seems like someone else's life now."

"And this Hoppin' John?"

"He was a handsome man. Well intentioned, I suppose. No, I know he was." Emily smiled. "He was crazy about Felicity.

"God, I wish you could have seen her in those days. She was so beautiful, she'd take your breath away. Johnny used to call her his Georgia peach. And that was right on target. Such a little bit of a thing, golden. Apricot-colored, really. Her hair that shade of ripe fruit, cut in a bob. And so fragile. Georgia peach was right. You were afraid to touch her for fear she'd blemish. Bruise." She paused for a moment. "They were the most incongruous couple."

"He was black."

Emily nodded. "Yes, he was. From New York. Different from any colored people *we'd* ever known. Talked fancy. Lord, I will never forget that man's clothes. He wore the most beautiful clothes."

Sam shut her eyes for a moment and watched Gatsby toss a great tumbled rainbow of his lovely shirts on a bed for Daisy. Choosing them, of all the things he was, of all the things he owned, to prove his worth to her.

"Yet, in other ways, they were so similar. They both had a kind of frenetic energy. Moved so quickly that sometimes all you saw was what they left behind, a sort of phosphorescent glimmer." She paused. "Am I making any sense?"

"Perfect sense. Go on."

"Well, there's not really much to tell. They met in the Little Club one night when Felicity stopped in after a performance, and fell head over heels in love. Felicity got pregnant."

"And Johnny?"

"He traveled. He was on the road. But, yes, he wanted to do the right thing by her. He tried to get her to marry him. But it was so ill fated. Felicity with her, *our* background. I'm afraid love doesn't conquer all. Though maybe it would have, but—" Her voice broke.

"What happened?"

"Johnny was on a tour through the Midwest. He called Felicity every night, begging her to join him, to marry him. She didn't know what to do. She was terrified. I'd come up and was staying with her. The phone would ring in the middle of the night. She kept saying she had to think about it. She was confused. And suddenly, there was silence. He never called again."

"Because she wouldn't say yes?"

"No, he literally disappeared. It took months for us to find out anything. You can imagine, Felicity was mad with worry. She thought he'd deserted her. And we couldn't get any word. The band kept traveling. Finally the story came, such as it was. He went out for a beer one night in St. Louis and never came back."

Was he crossing a rain-slick street? Did a speeding car bounce him up in the air and straight into heaven?

"They never found out what happened?"

"Never a trace. Nothing."

"What do you think?"

"I think he was killed. Johnny didn't have good sense when it came to lots of things. To Felicity, in particular. He carried a picture of her and loved to show it to people."

"So you think he bragged to the wrong crowd that this blonde was going to have his child?"

"Something like that. One can only surmise."

"And then?"

"When she heard the news, Felicity went into labor. She was about seven months along. It was easy to convince her the baby hadn't made it." Emily pushed at the tip of her aristocratic nose with a finger. "It seemed the right thing to do at the time. The only thing. Felicity was out of her mind. She needed to come home, to be looked after. And the baby—well, it was impossible."

"So you took the infant to her grandparents?"

"Ollie and James Jackson. They had met Felicity and were crazy about her, though they, too, were troubled by the relation—but in any case, they were delighted to have Margaret. She was all they had left of their only son, Johnny. They named her after his favorite grandmother."

"And then?"

"She grew up. She prospered. The Jacksons still had two almost-grown daughters at home, so she was lavished with love. Spoiled rotten. She seemed to inherit talent from both sides. She was singing and dancing on the stage of the Apollo by the time she was a teenager."

"So you kept in touch?"

"I sent a check once a year, and her grandmother wrote back, until Margaret was grown. Until she was through the Actors Studio."

"Where did she think the money came from?"

Emily smiled. "I doubt that she asked. Don't children just take whatever is handed to them? Think it's their due?"

"You're right. Of course they do. And her coming to Atlanta? That was just a fluke?"

"Entirely. She'd been with a rep company in New York for a long while. It came through Atlanta on tour and Margaret saw an opportunity here for building the kind of company she'd always wanted. And, with sheer grit, she did it."

"Not knowing about Felicity? About you?"

"Not until recently. A few months ago her grandfather told her on his deathbed that her mother hadn't died at her birth, which is the story she'd been told. He gave her enough information to lead her to me. To us." Emily shook her head. "Of course, she already knew us. Felicity had been a patron of the theater, on its board, since its founding."

"Then what?"

"She invited me to lunch. Confronted me. You see, she thought, from what her grandfather said, that *I* was her mother."

"Jesus. What did you do?"

"Well, at first I tried to bluff my way through it. It was awful. I didn't know what to do, and I had no warning. There we were, in the middle of lunch at the Ritz-Carlton, and out of the blue, Margaret starts screaming at me."

"She was angry, of course. Terribly hurt."

"She was *furious.* Unfortunately, what you don't know is that Margaret inherited her mother's manic-depression. And she can't drink at all. It sets her off onto wild tangents. She'd come well fortified that day. Had a couple of martinis and she was raving."

"What did you do?"

"The worst thing possible. I told her about Felicity. Somehow I thought if I told her the truth, everything would be fine. Why I didn't realize that it was far too late is beyond me." She shook her head. "I wasn't thinking. I felt so guilty. She got me in such a state."

"And?"

"She called me all kinds of terrible things, and then she stormed out the dining room. Oh, it was quite something." Emily laughed in spite of herself. "It's ridiculous, but I replay that scene again and again in my mind, and I always see it like something from a soap opera. Something I'd dismiss as nonsense and switch off."

"And yet—"

"And yet it's the stuff of our lives. My life and Felicity's."

"Then?"

"She went straight to our house. Felicity was home, puttering with her flowers or something, and Margaret barged right in, yelling at her, screaming. Felicity was aghast. She didn't know what had hit her."

"But she figured out who Margaret was?"

"She had no earthly idea. I mean, she knew Margaret, Margaret her friend, Margaret from the theater. But even after Margaret confronted her with the true facts, well, it made no sense to her. You see, Felicity believed that her baby had died over fifty years ago, in part because she wanted to. The next step was to repress the whole incident, the fact that the baby ever existed, Johnny, everything. Of course, when she's not doing well, bits of it pop out, wriggle through the seams, but most of the time it never happened. She's wiped that slate clean."

"Did you try to explain this to Margaret?"

"*Explain?* I couldn't explain anything. She'd already gone by the time I got there. Felicity was a lunatic. It took me days to get the story out of her. And Margaret wouldn't return my calls."

"But I don't understand. Now Margaret seems to be—you were at her party. Both of you. And Laura, her daughter—Jesus, Felicity's granddaughter—comes to Felicity for coaching."

"Yes." Emily smiled. "There was that horrible day, and then a silence, and then—poof! It was as if it'd never happened. Margaret still wouldn't talk with me, but suddenly one afternoon Felicity—who, of course, jammed that ugly incident away in a corner—said that Margaret had called and invited her to a dinner party. Had someone she wanted Felicity to meet. An old friend."

She gave Sam the nod, and Sam cocked a finger like a gun and named the name.

"Randolph Percy."

Seventeen

Sam was driving over to Sweet Auburn to the Players to find Margaret Landry. She wanted to talk with her. Now.

It was no coincidence that Margaret had introduced Randolph Percy to Felicity. She knew he was trouble. More than trouble. Percy was a weapon if pointed in the right direction. She'd wager Margaret had done more than that. She'd oiled and loaded him and slipped his safety.

The light changed and a horn behind her honked. She sped along DeKalb Avenue, a utility street, graceless, commercial, running beside the railroad tracks from Decatur into Atlanta, the same path that had transported Confederate soldiers in a vain attempt to save the city from the Yankees.

Okay. Margaret, angry as shit, fueled by gin, or maybe vodka, riding on the selfsame roller coaster of mania and depression as Felicity, introduces Percy to her mother. Then sits back and waits for him to kill her.

But he doesn't. He falls in love with Felicity—truly. And refuses to do her in.

Bullshit. He doesn't need to kill her because she gives him what he wants for the present, and maybe she's going to give him the rest in her will.

Fine. So what happened? How come Felicity's still doing fine and Percy's dead?

Felicity caught on and killed him first.

Or—Emily, who knew the whole story from the beginning, cut Margaret and Percy off at the pass.

Did Percy know what Margaret was up to?

Did it matter?

What else? Who else?

Ah, the lovely Laura.

And what was her role in this scenario?

Her mother told her about Felicity and Emily—the two high and mighty Miss Annes, denying her her birthright—not to mention a goodly fortune.

Laura helps her mother cook up the scheme for revenge. Whatever it is. But something goes wrong, and that's why Laura's at the Edwardses' house.

But Emily corroborated that Laura was there for a coaching session.

Well, of course, she had an alibi.

Sam ran that incident back through her mind. Laura at the door in her tennis whites. Laura awfully curious about what's going on with Felicity, trying to get past her to hear Felicity's and Emily's conversation. But she did get past her.

Sam let her go by herself back into the kitchen for a drink of water. And behind the kitchen was the pantry.

Of course!

Laura ransacked the pantry.

But that didn't fly. Laura came over on Wednesday afternoon. It wasn't until Friday, yesterday, that she and Emily had found the pantry pillaged.

Laura could have sneaked back later. Or Margaret, for that matter. Percy sure as hell hadn't. He'd been dead for two days.

Sam started. It was the damned cellular phone in her car. She'd never get used to it.

"It's Beau. Want to hear the latest on Percy?"

"Speak to me of the devil."

"Well, you know I told you that Mrs. Percy and the sister were camped out in my lobby?"

"Uh-huh." She was downtown now. She had to pay attention to traffic.

"So, when I released the body—they were ever so grateful—I went down personally, and Mrs. Percy started telling me how she'd urged Randolph—*Randy,* she called him—to go to the doctor. He'd been sick for a couple of days."

"How'd she know?"

"Seems as though he'd called her in Savannah. Momma's boy, I guess."

"Damn it! I knew that!"

"She told you?"

"She did. I wasn't paying attention because I didn't care about his health then. I was worried about Felicity's. She said he'd been feeling poorly."

"Well, she elaborated on it for me, and then I called the Claridge and got some corroboration from a steward there."

"And?"

"It sounds like flu. But flu didn't kill him, didn't develop into pneumonia like it does with a bedridden elderly person. Percy was in the pink of health, especially for his age."

"So?"

"This is what I've got. He complained to his mother that he felt dizzy. Sick to his stomach. He'd vomited a couple of times."

"But there was no vomitus with the corpse."

"Right. The vomiting was earlier. The steward said that on Tuesday night, Percy was complaining that his neck ached, felt weak. He was having some difficulty turning his head and more than a little trouble breathing. The steward tried to get him to go to a hospital, but Percy insisted it was only a flu bug and that he'd feel better."

"And he died the next day."

"Or sometime that night. Somewhere in that range."

"You think you know what it is, don't you?"

"Yes."

"So tell me, for Christ's sakes!" She veered into the left lane, narrowly missing a honking truck.

"Wait till I finish screening for it."

"Why?"

"I want to be sure. And trust me, Sammy. It's what I think it is, his death was accidental. Nobody ever murders anybody this way."

"People murder people every which way! And I'm inches away from who killed him. Beau, you can be such a Pollyanna!"

There was nothing but static for a minute. Then he said, "You know, Sammy, I put up with a lot of crap from you. But I think I've had about enough for this week. Why don't you go find yourself another M.E. to bother with your bullshit suspicions?"

Splat, slam, crackle. And then there was a dial tone.

Fuck him. She was way ahead of him on this anyway. Him and his super lab. Percy died accidentally? Horse shit. She could handle this like she handled everything else. By herself, thank you.

Eighteen

Margaret Landry sat by herself in her kitchen. Drinking.

She'd been at it for a couple of days now, lining up miniatures in a row like toy soldiers, then mowing them down.

The sweet ones were her favorite, peach schnapps in particular. It was cool and frisky at first, then warm and smooth in her tummy. Peachtree schnapps, actually, according to the label. How aptly named; her poison.

The thought made her smile.

The small bottles were best because she could hide them from Laura.

Oh, Laura knew she'd been drinking. She fussed at Margaret about it until she was red in the face—as if she were the mommy. But Laura couldn't stop her.

Not with these babies. She couldn't find the little bottles. Not in this apartment.

Margaret laughed at the idea.

Ho-ho-ho: her Santa Claus laugh.

She had played Santa Claus once at Macy's in New York when she'd been—what else was new?—in between shows and needed the cash. Laura was a toddler then—afraid of Mommy's white beard and mustache.

Laura would never find the cute little bottles in this jumble. Even in the kitchen, the shelves were piled high with scripts shoved in between her cookbooks, bowls, and Mason jars.

The rest of the apartment was a warren, passageways carved in among clothes racks jammed with costumes from the past ten, fifteen years.

Laura was always after her to get rid of them. Momma, why don't we clean this mess up? she would ask.

This was no mess. This was Margaret's life: slipping in and out of characters' skins, changing a bathrobe for a ballgown. That's what her life was all about.

Margaret twisted the top off another little bottle and held it up to the light. Inside the brown glass the liquid had no color. It could have been lots of things. Rubbing alcohol. Water. Cleaning compound. Peroxide—bleach your insides white as snow. You wouldn't know what it was until you put your tongue to it. Close your eyes. It was sweet—just like Margaret.

Don't kid a kidder.

Don't shit a shitter.

*Sweet*heart.

That's what Papa had called her: *my little sweetheart.*

But he'd been wrong, shitting her all that time. He and Big Ma, too. Didn't they know she'd catch on? Did they think that photograph of a high yellow woman they ran by her, *your poor momma,* tricked her for one minute?

Even as a child, Margaret had been nobody's fool.

She knew her momma was a white woman. What she couldn't figure out was why.

Why would her daddy, as handsome a brown-faced man as ever lived—and she knew those pictures were him—why would he choose a milk-pale woman like *her?*

Because *she* tricked him. That's why.

Lured him into her, spider to the fly. And then she killed him.

Oh, she knew how it had happened, Margaret did. She'd seen it all live and in technicolor in her own head. Just like an MGM movie in her own little theater, the one where she held private screenings. When she closed her eyes the picture came up and she'd seen that white woman seduce and abandon her daddy. And then abandon *her,* poor, helpless child.

She'd seen it all, just like she'd seen Miss Felicity die.

Emily, too.

Both those bitches toying with her like she was a fool, some witless fluff, some piece of rag and bone they could bat around for a while, then leave to die.

And the instruments of revenge, she'd seen those too in the movie.

She raised both her hands—smooth, light coffee, lots of cream— then flipped them over to the still paler palms. She'd seen her own fortune in them, scaring herself.

The instruments had come to her as if out of the sky.

Randolph Percy. That tongue-flicking snake. She could *smell* the evil in him.

When she'd said, "I have someone you need to meet," he hadn't even blinked. Thought he was so clever. Twinkling. Blue-eyed. But she'd wound him up and off he marched like a good little soldier.

She plucked another bottle now from the neat row. Twisted the top off. Sucked the sweet liquid.

Too bad he wasn't good enough.

Percy, Percy. *Tsk, tsk.*

What was she going to do now?

Maybe the *other* instrument's still there. Not a human one, and therefore more reliable. Sitting quietly on the shelf. Festering. Just waiting for a white hand, spotted with liver, to pick it up so it can reach down inside and kill her.

Maybe.

But better safe than sorry.

She'd have to go back.

It wouldn't be hard. Those *ladies* feeling so safe and sound in their world, the one they own, bought and paid for with the sweat off other people's backs. They were so easy to fool.

Just have to make sure the instrument works. No need to juice it up. You know what I'm saying?

You hear me, woman?

Momma, you hear me calling?

Can't you see that I was there?

Don't you know me, sweet momma?

Why, I left my calling card.

Don't you hear me knocking—knocking at your heart?

*   *   *

In the theater below Margaret's apartment, Sam parted a black velvet curtain at the back of the aisle and stepped into darkness. The only light was trained upon the lady. She was winding toward her end. The familiar lines were coming.

Lady Macbeth's hands writhed before her. "Out, damned spot! Out, I say! One; two; why then 'tis time to do't. Hell is murky!"

Was that Margaret?

The power was there, but it didn't sound like her contralto.

"Yet who would have thought the old man to have had so much blood in him?"

It was Laura. The understudy standing in for the lady at a Saturday matinee. Close to the end now. Sam had best get on with it if she wanted to see Margaret alone. That was probably the best way.

Sam slipped back through the black velvet into the light of the lobby, then out into the still brighter afternoon.

Margaret stiffened at the footsteps on the stairs. Her ears perked up, her eyes widened, then narrowed.

She was more than a little drunk, more than a little crazy. And once she was hidden, down deep in the dark, the humor fled her eyes, frightened off by the madness, which glittered.

The screen door screeched.

"Margaret?"

"Margaret, are you there? It's Samantha Adams. Do you remember meeting me?"

The door was open. Sam stepped inside, down a narrow black hall, feeling her way into the dark kitchen. All the shades were pulled in the apartment, blackout curtains. It was like night in here.

"Margaret?"

She could hear the nervousness in her voice, tinny in the stillness.

Well, shit. This was creepy. Smelled funny, too. The odor reminded her of something from her childhood. Maybe more recent. Something hot and sticky.

She felt along the walls for a light switch. Zero. She stumbled over a kitchen chair, bumped into a table. She rubbed her hipbone. That smarted. There'd be bruises to show for that lick tomorrow. Now she was in what had to be the dining room. More chairs and another table. An obstacle course of furniture.

She pushed forward.

"Margaret?"

Suddenly something brushed against her arm, then wrapped itself around her body. Panic climbed into her throat.

The thing was everywhere, touching her like a lover. Clicking. Long stringy things, clicking.

She got a handful of something now. Jerked at it. Something popped. Bouncing all around her. Jesus! It was a beaded curtain, its little wooden balls now rolling under her feet.

That's all it was.

Now you're scaring yourself shitless in the dark, Sam told herself. Get a grip on yourself. You need to think. Calm yourself.

She had to think.

Adams, you're making yourself stone crazy.

She had to concentrate now. Reach down and find a still place.

"Margaret? Are you in here? It's Sam Adams. I want to talk with you."

Ask you a few questions about whether or not you sicked Randy Percy on your momma.

Ask you whether or not you're a murderer.

Or, if you don't count Percy, an attempted murderer.

Ask if you've felt murder in your heart.

Sam was in a long hallway now jammed end to end with pipe-iron clothes racks.

She felt her way past can-can skirts scratchy with stiff crinolines. A woolly monk's robe brushed her arm. Something satiny slithered down a leg. Jesters' bells tinkled.

It was close as hell in here. She could hardly catch her breath, tried to slow it down. A surgical mask would be nice. It smelled like a swamp. Things rotting.

* * *

From her hiding place, Margaret watched through a crack. What did the woman want? What was she looking for? What would she take? Not good. Not good at all. Margaret was going to have to do something.

Sam saw a little light ahead. Must be the bedroom. Probably where Margaret was. Ill. Lying in her sickbed just like the girl at the box office told her a couple of days ago. Good. She wasn't above picking on Margaret when she was down.

Sam squeezed past the closet door. The ceramic knob carved across her back, bumped over her backbone.

She'd cleared it now.

She was reaching for the bedroom door. At least she could *see* something there.

In the dark behind her, the closet door opened.

A hand snaked out, then another hand. And suspended between them was a length of scarlet satin.

Then Sam was choking to death.

Margaret was a good five inches shorter, but she made it up in fifty pounds of heft, all coming down on the ends of the red sash—*from a pirate's costume, see Laura, how handy these old things are, kill this motherfucker burglar*—she'd thrown over Sam's head in one lucky move. Jerk. Snap.

Sam scrabbled at the sash with her nails, tearing her own flesh. She couldn't breath.

Step back, something told her. Step back into the force. Pull away and the noose tightens.

She stepped back. Margaret's soft bulk was like pillows behind her.

Sam went limp and collapsed onto Margaret and the choking sash, tumbling her over. The hands loosened now, flailed. Four arms and legs rolled in the darkness. Sam sat on Margaret. Bumped up against one another. Almost like love. But not quite.

"Kill you." Margaret grunted.

"Be still or I'll knock the shit out of you." Sam had one hand on

Margaret's gullet and the other arm drawn back. She wasn't kidding.

A whisper from the floor beneath her now. Stench of booze breath. "Who are you?"

"Sam Adams."

"Oh."

"Who the hell did you think I was?"

"Burglar." The word was slurred.

"Didn't you hear me calling you?"

She loosened her hold a little now. This was going to be all right.

"Please." Margaret turned, trying to curl into a ball. "Please don't hurt me," she said in baby talk. Then she pushed out an arm. "I hurt myself."

"I don't want to hurt you. You know I'm not a burglar, Margaret? You know who I am?"

Margaret's whole body nodded yes.

"If I let you up, you won't try to strangle me again?"

"I'll be good."

"Promise?"

"Promise."

They were sitting in the kitchen now, lights blazing. Sam had called the police, and was lucky enough to get Charlie. She got him to agree to hold Margaret for observation at Grady in the psych ward. She'd crashed into a box of Christmas ornaments in the closet, and had a mess of cuts on one arm, which was now wrapped in gauze. It would do as an additional excuse to hold her. An ambulance was on the way.

Sam had found the coffee, and was making a pot. Not that that would sober Margaret up. She should know. If you pour coffee in a drunk, you get a wide-awake drunk, that's all. There was no way she was going to get any answers now. She could do that in the hospital. But Sam needed the brew herself. She was still shaking. The scratches on her neck smarted. Coffee was the best she could do right now for comfort.

Margaret sat hunched in a purple robe. The color picked up the circles under her eyes. She didn't look good.

There was that smell again in the kitchen. Stale, hot, and sticky. Something about food.

"You cook a lot?"

"Yes." Margaret nodded. Perked up. Eager to please. "Are you hungry?"

"No, I just wondered."

Cookbooks were all over the place. Of course she did.

"I'll get you something to eat." Margaret was slurring only the tiniest bit now. She was coming back. She stood and headed toward the refrigerator.

Sam kept a careful eye on her.

"Sit down, please, Margaret."

"No trouble."

"I'm not hungry, really."

"Only take a minute."

She reached into the refrigerator, pulling out little bowls and plates.

"Please, Margaret."

The woman turned with a sad face. "Please let me. I'm sorry. I didn't mean to hurt you."

Well, hell. It couldn't hurt to humor her.

"Are *you* hungry?"

"I don't know."

"Okay. I'll take a little something if you'll join me."

Margaret beamed.

"But put it all on the table over here, if you don't mind." She didn't want Margaret diddling around with her back to her.

"Sure."

Piece by piece, Margaret spread a small feast before them.

"Cold leg of lamb. Here's some black bread. I made it myself. Hot mustard. And some relish."

She was fixing plates with little sandwiches for both of them, her broad hands busy and steady. She opened a Mason jar of marinated mushrooms and mixed it in with a relish.

"You like spicy things?" she asked.

Sam nodded.

Margaret grinned. It was almost the old Margaret. The original

Margaret she'd seen a week ago on the stage and at the party. The brilliant Margaret. The poor, deranged lady had almost completely disappeared. It was an amazing transformation.

"I'll put some Pickapeppa sauce on it, too. Is that okay?"

"Fine. I like hot things."

Margaret was finished now.

"There."

"Thanks."

Sam reached for the sandwich.

Margaret took a big bite of hers. "Oh, this is so good. I was so hungry." She laughed with her mouth full, then began choking.

Sam stood to help her, but Margaret waved her off. She pushed back from the table, then spit in the sink. Margaret filled two glasses with water and drank them down.

"Laura teases me about being too fond of my own cooking. I eat too fast. But I can't help it."

She drank more water.

Sam's sandwich was delicious. But the relish was very hot.

"Good," she said and nodded to Margaret, who smiled.

"You want a beer?"

"No, thanks. I don't drink."

"I do." Margaret giggled over her sandwich in her hand. "A lot."

"I know. Booze can get you in trouble. It got me in a lot of trouble."

"Really? Well, that's too bad." And then Margaret gestured, knocking her coffee into her plate. "Oh, shit. I'm a mess today."

"Here." Sam stood. "Let me help."

"No, no. Finish your sandwich. I'll get this."

Sam wolfed down the rest of the sandwich. She hadn't realized how hungry she was. She chased it with the hot coffee.

Margaret was listening now, her head cocked to the side. "I hear something downstairs."

Sam stood. "Remember, we agreed that you should go to the hospital for your arm."

Margaret pushed back from the table, the petulant drunk showing again. "I don't want to."

Now Sam could hear their footsteps on the stairs.

"It's going to be okay, Margaret."

"No, it's not. I'm not going." She settled herself into her chair. Well, they'd carry her out if they had to.

"Margaret, we can do this the easy way or the hard way. The hard way is going to be with a straightjacket, and you're not going to like it very much."

"Bitch!" Margaret was up and swinging now, lunging at Sam with a heavy arm, but she wasn't even close.

"Look out now." Sam was backing toward the door. She'd run for it if she had to. The boys were almost here.

Margaret stumbled backwards, fell into her chair, staring straight at Sam, but she didn't see her. Then she began reciting Lady Macbeth's lines. Her voice sounded like taffeta ripping. Sam had fought her own monsters when she was on the booze. She didn't want to know what was in Margaret Landry's head. But she had to listen anyway.

> I have given suck, and know
> How tender 'tis to love the babe that milks me;
> I would, while it was smiling in my face,
> Have pluck'd my nipple from his boneless gums
> And dash'd the brains out, had I so sworn as you
> Have done this thing . . .

Margaret faltered, then stood and paced. Her wide mouth began to quiver at the corners, to turn in on itself and hide.

"Babe. Poor baby."

Tears trickled down her cheeks, leaving a black track of mascara.

She stopped dead still before a long cabinet, its top littered with theater programs, ticket stubs, framed notices, and dried flowers. Her fingers brushed a framed baby picture of Laura. She picked up a loose snapshot, old and crinkled, and made a face at it. Sam moved a little closer. The woman in the picture was vaguely familiar, a beauty with a heart-shaped face and huge eyes.

Margaret spoke again.

Root of hemlock digg'd i' th' dark,
Liver of blaspheming Jew,
Gall of goat, and slips of yew . . .

Sam recognized the speech from Macbeth. One of the witches was giving a recipe for their poisonous brew.

Sliver'd in the moon's eclipse,
Nose of Turk and Tartar's lips,
Finger of birth-strangled babe
Ditch-deliver'd by a drab . . .

Margaret's voice broke. "Poor strangled babe. Fucking bitch." With that, the back door flew open, bouncing against the wall. Whew! It was the boys.

"Momma?"

Or was it?

"Momma? Are you here?"

Margaret ignored Laura, and went right on with her monologue.

"She *should* have strangled me, like that baby, strangled me at birth."

Margaret was pointing at the photograph.

Of course. Felicity. When she was young.

Laura saw Sam, and faced her with hands on hips. "What the hell are *you* doing here?" Still wearing her makeup from the play, she looked like Lady Macbeth but sounded just like her Great-Aunt Emily.

Before Sam could answer, Laura whirled toward her mother. She closed her eyes and took a deep breath.

Sam knew the feeling. But the horror was still going to be there when she looked again. It was going nowhere.

"I'm afraid—" Sam started.

Laura's eyes popped open. Her green gaze drilled Sam, then shifted to her mother and the debris on the kitchen table.

"Did you eat anything?" She flung the question at Sam.

"A sandwich."

"Shit! Goddamnit!"

What the hell was *this* all about? Sam had just about had a bellyful of this passle of crazy women—the whole bunch jerking her around for the past week. She pointed a hand in Laura's direction and counted off her gripes on her fingers.

"Look. One, your mother's drunk. Two, she tried to kill me. Three, I've got a bunch of questions I want to ask her about her friend Randolph Percy who's turned up dead. But in the meantime, we're taking her to Grady to observe her for forty-eight hours. In fact," she said and rotated her forefinger in the direction of the door and the footsteps now coming up the stairs, "that's got to be Emergency Services right there."

"Good." Laura's mouth was tight. Not nearly so pretty now. "You better ride in with them and tell them to pump your stomach when you get there." She didn't have to add *Miss Know-it-all.* Her face said that.

"Why the hell would I want to do that?"

"Your choice. No skin off my nose."

And there was the Laura that Sam had first heard talking with Miranda behind the potted palm.

"But I'm pretty sure my mom's just poisoned you."

Nineteen

Laura was right. Her mother had indeed spiked Sam's sandwich (as well as her own, which, of course, she didn't eat) with clostridium botulinum.

The attending physician said it for her very carefully after they finished with her in the emergency room, helping her puke her guts out.

Sam wasn't feeling too good at the time. She asked the doctor to repeat it when she dropped in to see her for a minute in the room where they were holding her for observation for twenty-four hours.

She got only half the term of Margaret Landry, who was without a doubt going to have to do a lot more time than that once she got out of Grady. Most probably in a nice warm psychiatric ward. Maybe somewhere out in the country.

Clostridium botulinum. She practiced it so it would go trippingly off her tongue when she said it to Beau.

He dropped by to see her.

"You wouldn't listen to me."

She said the two words she'd practiced.

"I know! That's what I was trying to tell you when you got so snooty with me on the phone."

"You knew that it was botulism?"

"I was screening for it when we talked. The only thing I could find that seemed at all out of the ordinary in Percy's autopsy was an excessive amount of fluid in the intestine. So I saved some, and then I kept running over what we had. The flu symptoms. Aching. Nausea. Vomiting. Difficulty breathing. Then I called Barnabas up at Quantico. He said he'd think about it, then called me back an hour later. He asked me if the old man had eaten any food that was canned at home."

"It was in the marinated mushrooms," Sam said.

"How'd she do it?"

"Came on it accidentally, Laura said. She's a great cook. Made batches of jam, did a lot of canning."

And in the process, produced that funny smell. Just a few weeks ago, Peaches had put up the last of some late tomatoes, and their kitchen had been filled with that hot, tinny odor, which was what Sam had remembered but couldn't put her finger on. She was going to have to ask Peaches how she'd guessed Margaret was Felicity's daughter. That had to be what Peaches had hinted at. *Infuriating* old woman.

"Did she get sick herself?"

"No, she knew what she had when a bunch of jars she'd lined in her cupboard began to pop. It sounded like gunshots in the night, according to Laura."

"And she gave a jar to Felicity?"

"Actually, she gave it to Randolph to give to Felicity."

"Pretty scattershot. She could have killed the whole lot of them."

"Which would have been fine with her. Felicity was numero uno, Emily a close second, and she was pissed off with Randolph because he wouldn't do Felicity."

"Did she ask him to?"

"I don't think so. She knew enough about him to know that he well might. But he seemed to be truly fond of Felicity, and besides, he was getting what he wanted for the present. But Margaret wasn't. She was growing mighty impatient."

"Laura told you all this?"

"Uh-huh. She sees that there's no way out for her mother but to come clean. Get her some help."

"And what was her role?"

"Nothing really. She knew her mother was getting pretty crazy, drinking a lot, so she'd tried to clean up behind her. She got wind of what Margaret was up to, listening to her drunken ramblings, so she went to the Edwards house to try to snag the mushrooms off the shelf."

"The day she showed up for her lesson."

"Right. The drink of water was an excuse to get back in the pantry."

"Where she smashed everything?"

"No. She was going to take the mushrooms. But she couldn't find them, so she came back later, sneaked in the house, and destroyed everything."

"Too late, though."

"Right. Percy was already dead then. Emily says Felicity had had Randolph over for tea Sunday afternoon. Among the things she served were the mushrooms he'd brought."

"But, you know, Sam, food contaminated with botulism tastes awfully rank. That's why more people don't die of it. And kids hardly ever. They just spit it out."

"Our Randy was a pig, according to Emily. She said she'd never seen a man tuck away so much food in her life."

"And you didn't taste it?"

"I thought there was something a little funny. But Margaret knew what she was doing. She piled on so much hot relish and Pickapeppa, I could have eaten—God, I don't like to think what."

"Well, they pumped you; you'll be all right. Did they give you antitoxin, too?"

"No. Blood tests showed I'm fine." She sipped the chocolate malt that Beau had brought her. "Did you screen the puppy?"

"Yeah. It was the same."

"Laura said it was a test to see if the toxin worked. Of course, it was a little torture for Emily, too. Playing with her."

"And the doll?"

"Right. And the chocolates and the Mother's Day card. She was pretty whacked out."

"Well. That's over, I guess, thank god." Beau stood, a little awkward now. "I've got to get back to the lab."

"Yep."

"No rest for the wicked."

"Right. Thanks for the malt."

"When are they letting you out of here?"

"In just a little while."

"Want me to wait? I'll give you a ride."

"Thanks, no. Nicole Burkett called." She pointed at a big bouquet of calla lilies. "She sent those and said she'd like to come by and take me home."

Beau whistled. "Tall cotton."

"I did her a favor once. My momma taught me it's nice to let people say thank you."

"Thank you for letting me pick you up," Nicole said as Sam slipped in beside her.

The back seat of the Rolls was deep and soft and wide. The partition between them and the chauffeur was shut tight.

"Thank you for doing it."

"I'm sure any number of people would have been happy to. Among them our Miss Wildwood. You must have quite a fan club."

"You're kind."

"I'm not. I'm honest. So I should tell you that I have an ulterior motive in mind."

They were floating up Piedmont in the Rolls. Past the turnoff to her street.

"We—"

"Humor me. This won't take but a few minutes. And then we'll get you right home to your family. I know they're all anxious to see you." Nicole leaned forward and opened the bar. "Would you like something cool to drink? A glass of water?"

"Yes. That'll be fine."

"Miranda has decided that she'd like to take a break from school." Nicole could have been making polite chitchat over lunch. "Europe is so lovely in the fall. She's been spending the past few days having long talks with a friend of mine, a psychiatrist who's not only awfully good, but awfully wise. He's helped me in the past." There was a long pause. "So I thought he could help Miranda. He suggested that the two of us might want to spend some time together. So we're going to Paris."

"Soon?"

"Day after tomorrow. We'll reopen our house there, spend a couple of months, come back for Christmas, and then Miranda can decide if she wants to go back to Scott or perhaps somewhere away from Atlanta."

"And your husband? He won't mind?"

"Yes, he will. But I'm not so concerned with his wishes right now. I've given him a wifely lecture about being more careful of his business investments. And I'm taking care of my daughter." She looked out the window for a moment. "I've talked with the mothers of all the other girls, too. They're handling things as they see best."

"His business investments?"

Nicole had just slipped that in. Surely she couldn't mean what Sam thought she did. Or could she?

"Are you saying that *your husband* is the owner of Tight Squeeze?"

Nicole made a small, neat gesture with both hands as if she were an umpire calling a runner safe.

"The property. Not the business. But the property."

"Good God."

Nicole nodded. "I think P.C. will be more judicious in the future." She turned and gave Sam a wide smile, ready to move on now. Old business. Finished. "That's all taken care of. Or will be soon. You agree with my decision about the girls?"

"Absolutely. I think you've done the right thing."

"Good. I thank you for your help. Now, you're feeling fine?"

"Right as rain. Just had a chocolate malt."

"Sounds wonderful." Nicole smiled.

Piedmont Park was on their right now. At Fourteenth, they turned left, then left again on Peachtree. Having described a long parallelogram, they were headed back toward home. What was the point of this little trip? Sam's eyes asked Nicole the question.

"Did you know," Nicole said as if she were answering it, "that the area around Tenth and Peachtree was called Tight Squeeze right after the War Between the States?"

Sam shook her head. George had threatened to tell her this story once. He never had.

"Why?"

"Though it was only a narrow dirt road then, it was notorious for being a hangout for thieves, vagabonds, and other thoroughly disreputable types."

Sam looked out the window, trying to imagine the busy street as Nicole described it. Nicole raised her voice to be heard over approaching sirens. Traffic stopped as a fire truck passed.

"There wasn't much here then. A blacksmith shop. A wagon yard. Maybe a few wooden stores."

Another fire engine. Sam put her fingers in her ears for a moment.

"But even so, so many scoundrels abounded that it was called 'Tight Squeeze.' "

A third emergency vehicle passed, wailing to beat the band.

"Because it took a tight squeeze to get through it?" Sam asked.

"Precisely. To get through with one's life."

Traffic was completely stopped now. They inched ahead. Three of Atlanta's finest had blocked the way with their patrol cars and were directing traffic to detour to the right.

"Some fire," Sam said, searching out the window for the blaze.

"Indeed." Nicole leaned across her and pointed. "There."

There was Tight Squeeze, or what was left of it. The fire was beautifully greedy, gobbling up the club. Orange flames shot high into the sky.

Sam looked back at Nicole, who smiled.

"Voilà," she said.

QUALITY PRINTING AND BINDING BY:
ORANGE GRAPHICS
P.O. BOX 791
ORANGE, VA 22960 U.S.A.